W9-ABN-030

CHAPTER ONE

Snow lay thick on the hills, glistening like a myriad diamonds under the light of a full moon floating in a clear purple sky. In the garden naked branches threw gaunt shadows across the lawn and the indeterminate borders where in spring and summer flowers and shrubs flaunted their brilliant colours. It was a night of sheer undiluted beauty, but this went unnoticed by the girl standing on the step.

She had gone to make sure the front door was safely secured, but on impulse had opened it instead, and now she stood there, gazing almost unseeingly at the slumbering white landscape, hushed and still beneath the brilliant winter stars.

From over a nearby hill there drifted the muted sound of children's voices and with a swift backward movement Dominie closed the door, turning the key and slipping in the bolt.

Christmas Eve ... Invitations had come in from anxious well-meaning friends, but Dominie had politely turned them down. Determined not to spoil anyone else's Christmas, she had said she was going to stay with a distant relative of whom her friends had never even heard, hence the suspicious questioning.

'You're not just saying this, Dominie?' from Hilary Fletcher, a friend from the office. 'You really are going to spend the holiday with this aunt?'

'I really am,' was the reply, and Hilary, like the rest, had to be satisfied.

'Hark, the Herald Angels Sing ...' The sweet tones

of the children were drawing closer and on entering the living-room Dominie snapped off the light, then sank into a chair and stared into the dying embers, her lip quivering tremulously. For two whole days she had wept; she felt she would weep for the rest of her life.

Minutes passed, and the clock ticked quietly on. Dominie shivered now and then, not with the cold, but at the memory of the ordeal through which she had so recently passed. Every nerve in her body tortured her, rioting madly as the mutilated face of her brother rose before her. Driven almost into a frenzy by it, she desperately began to pray. Peace ... oh, God, give her peace, if only for a few minutes. Her prayer went unanswered; she still saw her eighteen-year-old brother lying there, in the police mortuary. She alone could identify him, for they had no other relatives—except for an aunt about three times removed, whom Dominie and Jerry had never seen for over ten years. Jerry's face had been almost unrecognizable...

Shutting her eyes tightly, Dominie tried again to thrust the image out by thinking of other things, of times that had been happy despite the fact of her having been overworked, doing her job as wage-earner and in addition looking to all the household chores as well as being a mother to Jerry who was seven years her junior. Yes, they had been happy, those times she and Jerry had spent together. Dominie's boss, the manager of the large concern that manufactured electrical goods, had been most patient and understanding when his secretary asked for time off because her brother had to stay away from school owing to illness, or because he had broken his leg during the school sports. For one six-month period Dominie was off work over and over again, but never once did Mr Woodall stop her any money.

'Perhaps you'd better look for someone else,' she had said at last, though with fear in her voice. 'I'm not any good to you at all.'

'Just you attend to your brother, Miss Worthing,' he had told her kindly. 'You're doing a fine job of work, caring for Jerry and coming out as well. Many a one would look to the State to assist. If you can do your part, then I can do mine. I'll draw on the pool until you come back. Jerry'll not always be a child; one day he'll be bringing in money for you and then you'll find life much easier.'

And now Jerry was dead, killed instantly by the lorry which skidded on the icy road, careering across to mangle both motor-cycle and rider.

A great shudder passed through her body and she put her head in her hands, closing her eyes as if to shut out the agony that tormented her. And suddenly she was thinking of something else, something which tormented in a different kind of way. Those lost moments while she was driving home from the police mortuary ... that short blank in her memory. Often she had willed those moments to come back, but always she failed, and the blank remained.

Two years later she was telling Mavis Townsend about it. Mavis and her husband, James, had come to lodge with Dominie eight months after the accident, and the two young women had become firm friends.

'The only flash of memory is the screeching of brakes,' she explained as she and Mavis sat over breakfast before going to work. James had already had his and left the house, as he had to be at work by eight

7

o'clock. 'Apart from this I have a blank in my memory which I would very much like to fill in.' She was still affected by her brother's death, and her pallor was almost always in evidence. Although only twenty-seven, she often felt that she looked years older.

'You believe you had to pull up quickly for some reason?' Mavis obligingly showed interest, but it was plain to Dominie that she attached no particular importance to what Dominie had said. 'When was this?'

'On my way home from the police mortuary. I can't remember anything from leaving it until I reached the dual carriageway, which would take about a couple of minutes.'

'I expect such a thing is fairly normal, Dominie. After that shattering experience you wouldn't be able to think clearly, much less take notice of where you were going. In any case, when I'm busy with my thoughts I myself often have a blank when I'm driving. None of us consciously watches every stop or turn.'

Dominie was frowning.

'I feel that something happened—something important.' Her thoughts switched to that mortuary scene again. A kindly policewoman had come to her afterwards with a glass containing brandy. She was driving, Dominie had told the woman, but the glass had been pushed into her hand. Before she could put it to her lips, however, Dominie had been seized with such a fit of shivering that the liquid had spilled all down her coat. The car had reeked all the way home, Dominie recalled, and she had felt nauseated by the smell.

'I shouldn't worry,' Mavis was saying, intent on bringing Dominie from her brooding silence. 'Nothing at all serious could have happened, otherwise you'd have heard about it at the time.'

8

'That's true; but it is puzzling.' Dominie was frowning heavily, deep in concentration. What had happened during those few clouded moments? Mavis said it was nothing serious, and Dominie herself admitted this was probably so. Yet why this nagging worry that persistently recurred at intervals? Dominie sighed impatiently; she supposed the time would come when the matter would fade from her mind altogether.

'We must move,' said Mavis, glancing from the clock to the cosy glow of the electric fire. 'Why do people have to work? It looks so cold outside!'

'There's been a bad frost. I heard them gritting the roads earlier.' Dominie shivered; frosty days inevitably brought back the accident.

'I hope the buses aren't held up. I've been late twice in the last ten days. It's a good thing I have an understanding boss.'

'Same here. He was wonderful to me for many years. I was forever having time off when Jerry was at school.'

Dominie was once again to ask for time off, as the letter informing her that she had been left a legacy also requested her attendance at the office of the lawyers. She had received the letter a couple of days after she and Mavis had been talking about the accident, and Mavis was far more excited than Dominie.

'I hope it's a large one,' she said, having read the letter passed to her by Dominie. 'Small legacies are neither here nor there. You feel you must either spend the lot on something silly or else be sensible and put it in the bank. With a large one you can do both.'

'I can't think who has left it to me—unless it's that aunt I've mentioned. But she was always poor, and in any case, she hasn't communicated with me for over

9

twelve years.'

It transpired that the legacy had been left to Dominie by a Mrs Halliday, and it was quite a few seconds before Dominie could recall her.

'The old lady I used to speak to on my way home from work!' she exclaimed at last. 'She was always at her gate—weather permitting—and I would stop for a few minutes after getting off the bus. She lived alone and I was sorry for her. She seemed to spend her life standing there, watching the passers-by.'

The lawyer smiled.

'Well, Mrs Halliday was obviously grateful to you for giving her a little of your time. She made four such legacies to people who had been kind to her in her old age.' There followed some talk on the lawyer's part, about the legacy, and then he said, 'A thousand pounds is not such a bad little sum to come into unexpectedly, Miss Worthing. Have you any idea how you might use it?'

She shook her head, still dazed by this gift.

'I shall have to think. The most sensible thing would be to save it for a rainy day.'

'I shouldn't put it all away. Why not take a holiday? You've mentioned that you haven't had one for a long time.'

'Yes, I did mention that. You see,' she went on in a burst of confidence, 'my brother was killed in an accident two years ago and I haven't yet got over it properly. I've been advised by my employer to take a holiday, but I've felt I just couldn't.'

'How old was your brother?'

Dominie told him, and went further, giving the man a picture of her life after the death of her parents when she was only seventeen. They had both drowned when their small pleasure craft had capsized.

'You've had it tough,' frowned the lawyer, looking into her pale face. Her eyes held the sort of shadows bred by sorrow, and her mouth trembled as memory flooded in. 'Take a holiday,' urged the lawyer gravely. 'Why not try a cruise? Sea air's a wonderful tonic.'

A cruise ...

Mavis was all for it.

'James and I are going to Mum's for Christmas,' she reminded Dominie, 'so why not go away then? There are some marvellous Christmas cruises. I saw one advertised in Travelscene's window. It was to the West Indies.'

Christmas. Dominie dreaded it. Yes, it might be a good idea to go away at that time of the year.

The band played a rousing march as the huge white luxury liner moved slowly from the dockside at Southampton. Standing by the rail with dozens of other people, Dominie could not help feeling excited at the prospect of the cruise. It was for three weeks, and the liner was to call at several islands in the Caribbean— Barbados, Curaçao, St Thomas and several others. Yes, it was certainly exciting, and Dominie made up her mind not to think of that past tragedy, but to make a determined effort to enjoy her cruise.

But it was not easy, and she found herself thinking how wonderful it would have been had she been here with Jerry, sharing her good fortune with him. For he had had so little as a child; there had not been the money for presents which other boys had for birthdays and Christmas; there had never been any holidays by the sea.

'I say, I'm awfully sorry! Did I hurt you?'

Dominie winced but said with a smile:

'No, of course not.'

'I must have done, treading on your toes with my great clumsy foot.' The man, tall and broad, with fair hair and blue-grey eyes, spread his hands in a deprecating gesture. 'Forgive me. I have no excuse other than wanting to see the last of that band. They look so smart in their red and blue and white uniforms.' The man had an American accent and a pleasing smile. He stared down from his place by the rail and watched the departing band of musicians as they smartly moved along the quay, away from the ship which was now clear of the dock. 'Well, we're on our way. I wonder where those kids of mine have got to?' he added, obviously to himself.

Dominie watched his disappearing figure, allowing her curiosity to roam as she set to wondering about the children the man had mentioned, and about his wife who, it would seem, was not on the ship with him, since he had made no mention of her when murmuring about his children.

She was to meet him again very soon, as he was already seated at the dinner table when she was conducted to it by one of the blue-coated restaurant stewards.

'So we are to share a table for the trip?' He smiled and seemed pleased. The little girl beside him looked long and hard at Dominie, then glanced at her brother, who, sitting opposite to his father, gave a sideways glance, pursed his lips, then looked down, fidgeting with his fingers and softly whistling to himself. 'My name's Harris—Jake Harris, and these are my children. Susie's eight and Geoffrey's six.' He glanced swiftly from one to the other. 'Say hello to the lady.'

'Hello,' they said in unison, and half-grinned at one another.

'Hello,' smiled Dominie, taking up her napkin. 'My name's Dominie Worthing.'

'Nice.' Jake then added after glancing at her left hand, 'Miss, I take it?'

'That's right.' She wondered if this were one of the days when she looked years older than her years. It had all been such hustle and bustle at the end and she had become exceedingly tired.

'Are you English?' ventured Susie after a moment, and Dominie nodded.

'Yes, I'm English.'

'We're American, but we've been living in England, with Mummy. She's dead now, so we're going to live with Daddy all the time. You see, they were separated.'

Swiftly glancing at Jake, Dominie felt herself blush; she was embarrassed because of the child's outspokenness, and she felt sorry for the man. However, he merely grinned and said that there was no stopping the mouths of children.

'They just blurt out everything,' he added, taking up the menu. 'My wife had the custody of them, and as Susie's said, they lived in England, as she was English. She died three weeks ago, so here I am, bringing the kids to live with me.'

'We used to live with you before, though,' his young son reminded him, his shyness dissolving the moment Susie had spoken to Dominie. 'We lived with you for two months of every year.'

'I liked it. It's warm and sunshiny. England's cold and it rains a lot.'

'I live on the island of St Thomas,' Jake told Dominie, adding that his business was in New York and that he was away a good deal. 'I've to get a nanny for the kids,' he ended, and seemed not quite so cheerful all at once. Dominie could understand his anxiety and hoped he would manage to get someone suitable, someone who would understand the children, and be kind to them.

'You'll be leaving the ship at St Thomas, then?' she said, and Jake nodded.

'You're taking the cruise, I suppose?'

'Yes. I'm very much looking forward to seeing a few of the Caribbean islands.'

Jake gave a laugh.

'And seeing the limbo dancers, and listening to the steel bands?'

'That's right. Are the steel bands as good as they're made out to be in all the books one reads?'

'Indeed they are. You'll enjoy every minute of your visits to restaurants and night clubs. I see the shipping line has arranged quite a number of excursions for you.'

'They have, yes, but I haven't booked for any.' The cost had been so high that Dominie had hesitated about buying tickets, which she was urged to do by her travel agent, who warned her that she would not have the same chance of buying tickets if she waited until she was aboard.

'You've not booked? You should, first thing in the morning, as they soon get sold out.'

'Can you recommend any of the tours?' she asked, and Jake promised to go into the matter with her later, when the children were in bed.

'We'll arrange to meet somewhere at nine o'clock,' he began when Susie interrupted him, protesting that she wanted to remain up later than nine.

'So do I,' from Geoffrey. 'I want to go to bed when you go.'

'You're going at half-past eight. I shall have had quite enough of you both by then.'

Susie pouted.

'I shall tell Uncle Rohan of you!' she threatened sulkily.

'And probably get your backside smacked for your trouble, young lady! Uncle Rohan stands no nonsense, you should know that by now.'

'You have a brother?' It was some five minutes later that Dominie put the question, as they had all been busy with their food, choosing what they would have, and afterwards a small lull had settled on their table. Dominie spoke conversationally and a smile came from Jake in response to her question.

'No. Rohan de Arden's my nearest neighbour, and as he happens to love children mine are always at his place——'

'He likes little girls best,' interrupted Susie.

'He likes boys too!' Geoffrey glared at his sister across the table.

'Yes, he does—a bit. But he told me he likes little girls—not big ones. Only little ones.'

Amused, Dominie looked across at Jake, a query in her eyes.

'He's had a few rotten experiences where women are concerned,' Jake said, becoming serious and faintly thoughtful. 'However, to get back to what I was saying: he's my nearest neighbour and the kids call him uncle. He should have children of his own, as I'm always telling him, but he seems to have no interest in marriage.'

'He's French?'

'Rohan's a very attractive mixture. His father was French; his mother had an English father and an American mother. The result is that Rohan has a most interesting personality; and he's every woman's dream —as far as looks are concerned.'

'Yet he isn't interested in marriage. How strange.' Dominie was thinking more of the man's love for children than anything else, but on learning his age a moment later she did wonder how he had managed to escape the marriage net for so long.

'Thirty-four? You'd think he'd have been married long ago, seeing that he's so attractive. I mean—he could have anyone, by the sound of things.'

'No doubt about that. Women give him *that* sort of look all the time——' Jake broke off, grinning. 'You know what I mean? They find it difficult to be indifferent to his charms. But it gains them nothing; he's just not interested——'

''Because he only likes *little* girls,' intervened Susie, her mouth full of meat. She had been listening intently to the conversation, as had her brother, and Jake made a slight sign to Dominie.

'I'll tell you all about it later,' he promised, and from then on the conversation was such that the children could take part in it.

When the meal was finished Jake arranged to meet Dominie in the Calypso Room on the Promenade Deck and she was already there when he arrived, taking possession of the chair she had saved for him at a small table a little apart from the main body of people. She had brought with her the pamphlet describing the excursions, but Jake made no attempt to go through it with her at present.

'I'm exhausted with those two.' He leant back in his

chair, relaxed, and watched the dancers doing a fox-trot on the small space in front of the band. Dominie remained quiet, feeling he wanted it that way. His eyes closed now and then, as if he were tired. But, sensing her interest as she examined his rugged features, he opened his eyes and smiled at her. She liked that smile; it was sincere, friendly, inviting. He was a kind man, she thought, and, having previously assessed his age to be at least forty-five, she wondered how old he was when he married. He later told her his age was fifty-one, adding that he looked younger owing to the good life he had led. She laughed, as he meant her to, and told her he had been alone for five and a half years. 'We parted when Geoffrey was only a few months old,' he added with a note of regret in his voice. And he gave a small sigh. 'Just one of those things; it happens to so many couples these days. I sometimes wonder if that's one reason for Rohan's remaining a bachelor.' Jake stopped, and went quiet, as if considering, and then he shook his head. 'No, I'd rather put it down to his experiences. His mother had a raw deal, being supplanted in middle age by a lovely young thing of twenty-two who managed to hold on to Rohan's old man until he died and so got most of his fortune. Rohan's mother died a few years before her husband, kept in luxury by Rohan, who had entered business when quite young and made a phenomenal success of it. He's now a millionaire.'

'So Rohan had a hate at an early age, apparently?'

'He certainly hated that girl. Then about five years ago he began going around with a beautiful brunette whom all the men raved over. She and Rohan seemed eminently suited in every way, but she met a man even wealthier than Rohan, and this, plus a title, resulted

17

in the break-up of the affair just as we all expected an engagement to be announced. Most people felt sure he was in love with Nina...' Jake broke off slowly, his brow creasing in thought before, dismissing whatever it was that had caused the frown, he gave a small shrug. 'Nina doesn't live in St Thomas, which is a blessing. Rohan hasn't seen her since her marriage and to all outward appearances he has got over it.'

'He should have, in five years.'

'One never can tell with love.' Jake looked curiously at her. 'You haven't a young man?'

'No.'

'I concluded that. You wouldn't be taking this cruise if you had.' His tone invited her confidence, but she refrained from entering into explanations about her life. Instead, she reintroduced the subject of Rohan de Arden, saying it was understandable that he should dislike women, but adding that there were other types besides those who had caused him hurt.

'Perhaps.' Once again Jake took on a musing attitude. 'I haven't told you all,' he went on after a while. 'You see, he had a young sister to whom he was greatly attached. He was her guardian, but allowed her to go to England to be trained in acting, as that is what she had wanted from being quite small. Rohan has friends in England, and they had Alicia living with them. Well, Alicia had great talent and by the time she was twenty she had made two films. He went over often, as she was on television and liked him to see her. He brought her over to St Thomas for holidays and on the particular occasion in question he had gone over for that precise purpose, as it was Christmas time—just less than two years ago, as a matter of fact.'

Two years ... Dominie clenched her fists, forcing

herself to thrust the tragedy from her. She looked at the band, at the couples dancing, at the people sitting around, talking and drinking.

'What happened?' she heard herself say, still fighting to shut out her brother's face.

'Rohan had hired a car to take them to the airport; there was an accident and Alicia was killed——'

'Killed! Oh, how dreadful!' Dominie's fingernails were biting into the palms of her hands. How could she forget her own anguish when here was Jake, talking about another death ... and one that had occurred almost at the same time as Jerry's?

'Yes, it was a terrible thing—a great blow to Rohan. A woman driver came out of a minor road—raced out, in fact, without even slowing down or sounding her horn. Rohan tried to avoid an accident by swerving, but hit a lamp standard. The girl drove a short way, then stopped, but only long enough for a witness to pop his head through the window and discover that she was drunk. She then started the car up and drove away.'

'But how wicked! Wasn't she jailed?'

'They never found out who she was. The witness said she reeked of whisky, or some spirit. And she blabbered something unintelligible before driving away. It was dark and the man couldn't get her number. Rohan was a broken man when he returned home, and I do believe that he would have killed the woman, could he have found out who she was.' Jake stopped, noticing the pallor of Dominie's face. 'Is something wrong?' he inquired anxiously.

'My brother was killed two years ago—just a couple of days before Christmas. Rohan's sister must have been killed about the same time.'

'Your brother? I'm terribly sorry, Dominie. I wouldn't have spoken of such a matter had I known how it must affect you. It's brought it all back, I suppose?' He asked the question unnecessarily and instantly apologized for doing so. 'My dear child, forgive me——'

'You're not to blame,' she hastened to assure him. 'You couldn't have known about my tragedy.'

'No . . .' Jake lapsed into one of his thoughtful moods. 'What a strange coincidence,' he murmured at length, 'that your brother and Rohan's sister should die about the same time, and both in road accidents.'

'Yes, it is—a most strange coincidence.' Dominie paused a moment. 'It's understandable now why Rohan hates women. Just think—that young girl, cut off from life just as she was becoming a great actress.'

Jake nodded.

'She was very beautiful, too, and charming. We all loved her dearly.' Once again Jake became thoughtful, but suddenly he rose and reached for Dominie's hand. 'Come, let's dance! We're not going to talk of such matters again!'

For the rest of the evening they danced together, or sat with their drinks watching others on the floor. At midnight there was a floor show and immediately it was over Dominie said she was going to bed. Jake, who several times had left her to go and see if the children were all right, said he too was ready for bed, and they left the Calypso Room together, having spoken for a time to the couple at the next table, who also had two children of similar ages to those of Susie and Geoffrey.

'Perhaps we can get together regarding the baby-watching,' Dorothy had suggested, for her husband was also making journeys now and then to their family cabin two decks below. 'We have a party to attend, and if you could see to our two, we would see to yours if you wanted to go ashore at Barbados on Wednesday evening?'

'Certainly. We'll discuss it later.' Jake had been into the question of excursions with Dominie, but as he and she walked away from Dorothy and Vic he suggested they should go ashore at Barbados together.

'Let me take you to the Hilton for the barbecue and the show. We can dance afterwards. You'll love it there.'

'Thank you very much,' returned Dominie. 'It's most kind of you to ask me.'

'Nothing of the sort. I'm considering myself lucky to have found someone so pleasant—and attractive,' he added with a fatherly sort of smile.

'Thank you,' she said again, this time rather shyly. 'I also am lucky.'

'If I'm not too old, and I don't bore you or cramp your style, I'd like to be your companion until we reach St Thomas. May I, Dominie?' They had reached 'A' Deck and Dominie had stopped, as her cabin was just around the corner from where they were standing.

'I'd love that,' she responded enthusiastically, her mind calculating, and telling her that by the time they reached St Thomas the dreaded date would be past. 'I shall feel glad of your company, Jake.' These last words spoke volumes and he nodded understandingly.

'Just treat me like a father,' he said, and touched her cheek lightly with his lips.

CHAPTER TWO

THE ship docked six days after leaving Southampton and Dominie and Jake went off in a taxi to the Hilton where they ate outside among the trees and later danced to the steel band. Limbo dancers performed for them, and later still Dominie and her companion strolled along the beach, with the warm waters of the Caribbean lapping the shore and the sky above star-studded, and spangled here and there with soft white cloud.

'It's so warm. You'd be able to swim in this sea—even now, at midnight!' Dominie was bending down, her hand in the water. 'Just think ... it's December!'

'You're in the tropics, my dear,' Jake reminded her in his soft American voice. 'It would be very strange if it wasn't warm. We could have rain, of course,' he thought to add, glancing up at the sky.

'I'm glad we haven't had it. It was fun being outside all the time.' She straightened up, coming closer to Jake than she expected, for he had moved towards her. He took her hand, drying it with his handkerchief.

'You're a nice kid,' he said, looking into her face. 'Why haven't you found a young man before now?'

She watched him with the handkerchief, recalling that last evening at dinner she had told him her age.

'There wasn't much time for going out,' she explained after a small hesitation. 'I was looking after Jerry, and there was such a lot to do in the house. I never met any men—apart from those I saw at the staff dance and at the odd party given by my friends.'

'You don't mind not having a young man?' He put the handkerchief away in his pocket, but retained her hand in his.

'No, I don't mind. I'm a fatalist, and if I'm to marry, the right man will appear ... from somewhere,' she ended vaguely, and with a little laugh.

'You're right,' he agreed with a sign. 'Yes, you're right.'

She withdrew her hand, but made no move to walk on. They were right on the edge of the shore, with the gentle sea moving ever so slightly at their feet. A breeze came over the water—the cooling north-east trade wind—and fanned their faces. She looked up at Jake, sensing that he was sad. He seemed to know this and presently told her that he had been very much in love with his wife right up to the time of parting.

'I don't know whose fault it was——' Jake broke off, frowning and shaking his head. 'Perhaps it was mine. I believe women like a masterful man and I'm not that sort. I'm always afraid of hurting people. I suppose I'm not manly enough.'

'Of course you are!' exclaimed Dominie indignantly. 'You shouldn't say that!'

'Thank you, my dear. What a nice girl you are.' He smiled as she blushed in the half-light thrown off by the lamps in the trees. 'But to get back to my wife: she was not happy for a long while before she suggested we separate. I felt she was—well, ashamed of me.'

Dominie gave a little gasp.

'That's impossible!' Her eyes travelled from his rugged kindly face to his hair, fair and wavy and clean. She looked at his immaculate attire, at his broad shoulders squarely set. 'How could you possibly have gained an impression like that?'

'I didn't mean ashamed of my personal appearance, Dominie. I meant that she was not proud of me as a

23

man. If you saw Rohan you'd know what I mean.'

'But he's one in a thousand, from what you've said. It's the same with women—you get one now and then who is superlative, flawless in every way. That doesn't mean that all the others are to be despised. And anyway,' she added, the note of indignation creeping once more into her voice, 'this Rohan might not have such a nice personality as other men. They haven't, usually, when they're so admired, you know.'

Jake was smiling, with humour. She was talking about one of his best friends, he said, and Dominie gave a small start and hastened to apologize.

'How could I forget that? I'm terribly sorry,' she said again.

'Don't worry, my dear. It's not important.' His blue-grey eyes twinkled as they rested on her flushed cheeks. 'I've said, don't worry about it.'

'I didn't stop to think,' she murmured, biting her lip, 'or I would never have spoken disparagingly about your friend.'

'He'll be looking forward to seeing the kids,' said Jake, veering the subject a little, for Dominie was still embarrassed at her lack of tact. 'And I expect he'll be glad that they're to stay permanently with me.' Dominie said nothing for a while and they began to walk on again, along the quiet shore. From the hotel gardens behind drifted the sounds of the steel band, and the heady scents of tropical flowers.

'Is St Thomas as lovely as Barbados?' she asked at length.

'We who live there consider it even more lovely. There isn't the poverty, for one thing. Here, you have a great gap between rich and poor. St Thomas is U.S.-owned and the standard of living is high.' He paused a moment, drifting into his familiar mood of thoughtful silence. 'It's a great pity you're not staying longer at St Thomas; I could have shown you round.'

'I'll book an excursion; at least I shall then see a little of the scenery.'

Jake nodded, again thoughtful.

'The ship's scheduled to stay for nine hours, I believe?'

'Yes, that's right. We arrive at nine in the morning and leave at six in the evening.'

'Not long enough,' he asserted with a frown. 'It'll take you an hour to get organized on your trip. You've to come ashore by launch, remember, and then there's sure to be a delay in leaving Charlotte Amalie Harbour. Pity,' he said musingly, 'great pity you'll not see more of our beautiful island.'

'None of these stays are long enough. I could stay in Barbados for a week. But we've been given only a few hours.'

'Badly organized—all these cruises are. You travel for six whole days to get to the Caribbean, and once here you stay for so short a time that you scarcely get a proper impression of a place. It's such a shame, for every one of these islands is a tropical paradise.' They were still strolling along on the beach, but Jake glanced at his watch and said that, pleasant as it was, they must retrace their steps and get a taxi back to the ship.

'I've had a wonderful evening,' Dominie was saying when at last they were back on board the great white liner. 'Thank you very much, Jake.'

'Thank you, my dear, for the pleasure of your company.'

'Well, here we are, Dominie.' Jake spoke with a distinct hint of regret as he and the children sat down to breakfast on the morning after Boxing Day. 'This is where we say goodbye.'

Dominie felt strangely choked; she had become fond of Susie and her brother, and she had also enjoyed immensely the company of their father. He was a thorough gentleman in every way, grateful for her company, and showing this gratitude in many ways. At Curaçao he had insisted on buying her a bracelet despite her vigorous protests. The children supported him and in the end Dominie gave way, and now she owned a piece of jewellery she would never even been able to buy for herself.

'You've helped with the kids,' Jake reminded her in the midst of her protests, 'washing and ironing all their clothes like that.'

'It was nothing. I had to do my own, so it wasn't any trouble at all.'

'We want you to have that bracelet,' from Susie. 'It's beautiful—real gold!'

'It'll look nice, Auntie Dominie,' supported Geoffrey with enthusiasm. 'My mummy had hundreds of bracelets like that!'

'Not hundreds, Geoffrey,' chided his father. 'Don't exaggerate.'

Dominie wore the bracelet now, and as she glanced at it she felt a great surge of dejection that she would never see Jake again, or the children. He had confided that when his wife died his feelings were mixed. His hopes of a reconciliation had long ago been crushed and he had unhappily accepted that his children were denied to him for all but two months of every year. Although he felt sad at the death of his wife, who was seventeen years younger than he, he was at the same time happy at the prospect of having his children to live with him on the island. He owned a house in the hills, he said, but made no other mention of it, and Dominie was left guessing as to what it was like. Susie had mentioned a swimming pool and Geoffrey a tennis court, so she assumed it was a luxurious place.

'Why,' said Geoffrey right out of the blue, 'can't Auntie Dominie come home with us? It doesn't take long in the car, and then we can come back and wave to her as she goes away to the ship.'

Jake said quietly,

'I've already thought of that, Dominie, but I didn't mention it because obviously you want to make the most of your visit here. Unfortunately I must get home to attend to my mail, otherwise I could have spent the day with you and gone home later.'

'Please come,' urged Susie, her brown eyes pleading. 'I want you to.'

'I'd love to have you for the day.' Jake looked at Dominie across the table, 'My work will take about an hour, but after that I could give you all my time. We could take a trip in the car, so you would at least see a little of the island, though not so much as if you took the excursion.' He paused a moment and then, 'The offer's there, my dear; it's up to you to accept or reject it.'

She accepted, suddenly deciding that a forfeiture of her sightseeing was preferable to being on her own all day. True, there would be others in the mini-bus, but they would be strangers to her.

They all left the ship half an hour later, by launch, landing at the capital of Charlotte Amalie.

'How wonderful to be setting foot on American

soil!' Dominie was excited, and it showed. Her cheeks, so often pale, were flushed, and her blue eyes shone with that violet light which was seen only when she was happy. Her fair hair, short and curled, gleamed like gold in the sunshine pouring down from a tropical sky. She glanced about her; the land rose all around the harbour, lush and green; palms swayed against the sky where fleecy white clouds hung suspended against the background of vivid blue. Many small boats were in the harbour and a little way out four huge luxury liners were anchored. Hassel Island lay dreaming in the harbour—two low hills, green-clothed and fringed with buildings. A native sloop drifted serenely towards the spot where Dominie was standing; she smiled at the occupants and they responded with waves of the hands. Cars of breathtaking size swept along the waterfront; exotic trees flaunted their brilliant crimsons and yellows and pinks. 'It's beautiful,' breathed Dominie, turning to Jake and noting to her surprise that he was frowning. 'Is anything wrong?'

'My car should have been here, with the driver. Now what can have happened?'

After waiting for about a quarter of an hour Jake called a taxi. It was driven by a native driver who, smiling broadly, opened the doors for them and said with a pronounced American accent,

'Sunset Lodge, in quick time!'

'He knows you?' Dominie, in the back with the children, spoke as the car pulled away.

'It's an island,' was all Jake said, and it was only later that Dominie learned that he was one of the wealthiest men on St Thomas.

'You've been here before, lady?' The driver spoke

over his shoulder as he took a turning off the water-front road known as Veterans Drive.

'Never,' she replied.

'Then you're in for a treat.'

'Miss Worthing's come from the cruise ship, as you've probably surmised,' put in Jake, leaning back in his seat. 'It's her first visit to the Caribbean.'

'Ours is the best island of them all,' asserted the driver, whose voice vibrated with pride. 'American! They know how to do things, you see, and so we're all very happy here!'

'You're an American?'

'Of course.' He fell silent a moment and then, his tone changing to one of faint disgust, 'Didn't I tell you that the Americans know how to do things? See these holes in the road? We make a hole one day, fill it in, nicely pave over it, then the next day we dig it all up again to lay another pipe. The Americans just love to see holes in the road!'

Dominie laughed and said,

'We appear to have that in common. The British also love to see holes in the road.'

'They do?' with surprise. 'You mean, they just go on digging up the roads, mending them, then they start digging them up again?'

'That's right.'

'Crazy,' laughed the driver, who after a small silence told Dominie to call him Joe. 'Is the lady wanting a taxi back to the ship?' he then inquired of Jake.

'No, thank you. I shall take her myself in the car.'

'Okay. I just thought I'd ask, as then I would make sure I'd be free. I thought you'd have had your car waiting for you when you got off the ship,' he added on a curious note.

'It should have been there to meet the ship. I can't think why it wasn't.'

The car was now climbing the mountain road, its sinuous route taking them to the other side of the island, and with every hairpin bend came another magnificent vista of breathtaking beauty. Far down below the numerous islands and islets and bays that surrounded St Thomas could be seen. They were all volcanic peaks, tops of mountain ranges buried under the waters of the ocean.

'That's Tortola, one of the British Virgin islands,' Joe said, pointing downwards to the sea. 'The one near to it is Jost Van Dyck.'

'Are some of the small islets uninhabited?' inquired Dominie with interest.

'That is so, lady. There is one that's uninhabited, but it's cultivated——' Joe broke off to point out the red hibiscus hedges and the magnificent Royal poinciana trees blazing along the roadside. 'We have a good rainfall and so we call this Paradise Island!' Jake glanced back at Dominie and smiled as Joe said this. On Barbados the taxi driver had given the island the same name!

The taxi slowed down at last, and entered between the high wrought-iron gates. The house came into view and Dominie gave an audible gasp. She said, in a voice that was little above an awed whisper,

'I had no idea, Jake...' She had been going to say she had no idea he was so very wealthy, but stopped as Jake laughed. How modest he was! No mention had been made of all this splendour.

The house, low and white, spread over the magnificent grounds where exotic trees and bushes grew in numerous colourful clusters. The swimming pool shone brilliant blue and she later learned that it was illuminated from underneath at night.

'Well, Mr Harris,' observed Joe as he slid from the taxi and opened the door, 'Paul doesn't seem to be here.'

'No. I expect he arrived late at the quay and is now on his way back. It's a wonder we haven't seen him on the road.' There was no sign of anger in Jake's voice; he seemed to have decided there was some good reason for his chauffeur's non-appearance at the quay.

With Joe paid off the four entered the house, being met at the door by a native servant who took Jake's luggage away. 'We'll have some coffee and then I'll leave the kids to show you round for an hour until I'm free.' Jake rang a bell and Molly appeared, a welcoming smile spreading over her dusky face. She eyed Dominie, then looked curiously at Jake. 'Miss Worthing's come to stay with us for a few hours,' he explained. 'We'd like some coffee, please.'

'Yessir! I will fetch it at once.'

'Do they all speak such good English?' Dominie wanted to know in some surprise.

'English is the language here. The locals do have a patois—a West Indian dialect which is a hybrid of French, Spanish, German and Dutch, the result of the slave-traders' endeavours to teach their workers to speak European languages. But this patois has been substantially modified by English in recent years.'

'Everyone seems so happy and content.'

'Of course they are. This is an affluent society in which almost everyone has a share.'

Dominie sat down, while the children ran off into the garden and Jake leafed swiftly through the heap of letters he had taken from the table in the entrance hall. The room was white and gold, with crimson carpet and drapes. Everything was modern, and expensive. From his place at the open french window Jake said, glancing up from his correspondence,

'This is going to take rather longer than I expected, Dominie. I've to make several long-distance calls, and wait for some answers.' He gave a small sigh. 'This is what comes of being away; there's always a great deal of work to catch up with on my return.'

'Don't worry about me, Jake. I shall be quite happy just looking around your beautiful gardens.'

'Thanks, my dear. We'll have our coffee together and then I'll see you again at lunch-time.'

Paul arrived during the afternoon, having previously telephoned to say that the car had broken down and he was having it repaired at a garage in Charlotte Amalie, to where he had had it towed from the mountain road. Jake had been forced to stay in anyway, owing to the necessity of receiving the answers to his calls. It was rather late to go for a run, Dominie thought, and although Jake plainly regretted her missed opportunity of seeing something of the island he was just as plainly relieved by Dominie's attitude. She convinced him that she had thoroughly enjoyed herself, going round with the children and then playing ball on the lawn.

'We've had a swim as well,' she informed him. 'Susie found me a bikini from somewhere.'

'My sister left it a few months ago when she came on a visit from Florida, where she lives.'

All too soon the time for Dominie's departure arrived. She felt inexpressibly flat and depressed, but was at the same time grateful for the company she'd had during those days when the tragedy of her brother would inevitably have occupied all her thoughts. She said goodbye to Molly, who wished her a safe voyage home, then went with Jake and the children towards the car.

Ten minutes later Jake was shaking his head as he pressed the starter for the last time.

'It's no use; the darned thing isn't going to start. Whatever was wrong with it hasn't been put right, obviously.'

'Can't Auntie Dominie go back to the ship?' asked Susie with undisguised delight. 'Will she have to stay with us?'

'Uncle Rohan will take her,' answered Jake quietly, opening the door for Dominie to get out of the car. 'I'll phone him at once.'

'Rohan?' Dominie looked swiftly at Jake as she stepped from the car. 'Won't he mind?'

'Not at all,' replied Jake with confidence, and strode away towards the house.

But Rohan wasn't in, and although Jake telephoned immediately for a taxi half an hour passed and it failed to arrive. Meanwhile Rohan had returned and, receiving the message from his servant, drove over at once to Sunset Lodge.

Dominie and Jake were on the terrace and they hurried to the car; within seconds she was being introduced to its owner.

'How do you do,' murmured Dominie, stunned by his magnificence despite the description she had been given by Jake. She was unable to take her eyes from his face, a proud face but strong of line and feature, a face that was an expressionless mask at present as Rohan de Arden stared down into Dominie's wide blue eyes. She noted the angular jaw, prominent and set, the firm yet

33

sensuous mouth, the black hair forming a slight wave at each side of the peak that cut into the low and faintly-lined forehead. His eyes were of an unusual colour—a sort of dull amber which, with the sudden appearance of Susie who came running from the house, changed and became alive.

'Uncle Rohan!' Susie would have flung herself into his arms, but her father took her hand and pulled her away, saying,

'Rohan, the ship sails at five——'

'Five!' Rohan glanced at his watch. 'Get in, Miss Worthing,' he said, and within seconds they were on the road.

She was taking her last look at the beautiful Magens Bay when she heard the exclamation from the hitherto silent driver, and she turned her head. Before them, just on the hairpin bend, were two cars which had obviously collided with one another. The occupants appeared to be unhurt, for they were standing around —but the road was completely blocked.

Getting out of his car, Rohan helped to move one of the cars, but it took a good deal of time and when at last the quay came into view the ship could be seen, just moving away from where it had been moored in the bay. Rohan stopped and turned, noting Dominie's pallor and the drawn expression on her face.

'You'll have to fly out to the next port of call,' he told her casually. 'Where is it?'

'Martinique,' she quivered, unconsciously gripping her hands together. 'All—all my luggage is on board.'

'I expect it is,' with faint sarcasm. 'When does the ship reach Martinique?'

'Ten o'clock tomorrow morning,' she replied flatly, 'and it leaves twelve hours later.'

He gave a careless shrug and said,

'You can't get a flight at that short notice. What other places does the ship call at?'

'None until it reaches Madeira a week today.' Her lip trembled. 'I'll have missed half the cruise,' she murmured to herself.

'Bad luck.' Rohan spoke with the same careless intonation to his voice. Plainly he was not interested in her, or concerned in any way about her plight. 'However, there's nothing to be done. You'll have to rejoin your ship at Madeira.'

Jake was full of apologies on their return to Sunset Lodge; his anxiety, and the way he looked at Dominie, brought a curious gleam to Rohan's eyes, and he glanced from Jake to Dominie several times, pursing his lips.

'Did it never cross your mind that you could call a taxi?' he asked of Dominie in smooth and even tones.

'Jake called one, but it didn't arrive.'

'I see. It would almost seem you were fated not to catch your ship.'

Dominie glanced indignantly at him. His indifference was almost inhuman. Anyone with any feeling at all would have expressed sympathy, even though she was a stranger. Jake was speaking, telling Dominie not to worry too much, and promising to arrange her flight to Madeira.

'It mightn't be too bad, my dear,' he added, smiling in a quiet reassuring way. 'I'll see that you enjoy yourself while you're on the island.' His eyes strayed momentarily to where Rohan was standing, looking decidedly bored with the entire business of the missed boat. 'You'll be quite happy here,' Jake added swiftly as he saw that Dominie was also looking up at Rohan, and noting the expression on his face.

Jake was right. After the flight had been arranged Dominie managed to relax, and to enjoy her stay on the lovely Caribbean island. Stowed away in one of the spare rooms were two large trunks, full of clothes which had been left behind when Jake's wife went off with her children to England, and on going through these Dominie found that many were suitable for her to wear despite the fact of their being rather large. Jake's wife must have been less slender than Dominie, and a little taller. However, the clothes were very welcome, and as there were several pairs of shorts and sun-tops she was able to sunbathe, adding to the tan she had already acquired on the ship coming over.

'I'm giving a party,' Jake told her one afternoon when they were having tea on the lawn. 'We have lots of parties here. About a dozen people will be coming, and if you can't find a suitable dress I hope you'll allow me to buy you one.'

She shook her head, saying instantly that there was sure to be a dress she could wear.

'I couldn't let you buy me one,' she added even though Jake frowned a little. 'You're being most kind as it is. This visit of mine must be inconveniencing you immensely——'

'On the contrary, it's giving me nothing but pleas-ure, Dominie. I hope you're enjoying it as much as I?'

'Indeed I am,' she returned with swift enthusiasm. 'To be frank, I'd much rather be here than on my own on the ship.'

'Thank you, my dear.' Jake glanced up as Rohan came striding across to where they were sitting, under a breadfruit tree, their afternoon tea spread daintily on a table before them. 'Hello, Rohan! You're just in time for a cup of tea.'

'Thanks.' He eased his long body into a chair and stretched his legs out in front of him. 'I just called to see if I could bring a friend along to the party this evening. She and her parents flew in today and called unexpectedly. I do a great deal of business with Mr Fortescue, and naturally I've asked them to be my guests for a few days. They'd booked in at an hotel, but I couldn't have that.' His voice, usually low and casual, took on a note of authority and Dominie felt that if he told someone to do something, then they would do it, without question. 'The Fortescues are island-hopping by plane. The trip's a silver wedding present from Tom to his wife. Sylvia has come along too and I'd like to bring her this evening if I may.'

'But of course! Bring them all.'

'Tom and Dora prefer to stay in and have a rest. They've had several late nights, they tell me, and are happy to make themselves at home and just sit and listen to some music.'

'Well, the invitation's there if they wish to accept it.'

'I'll tell them, but I don't think they'll come.'

Another cup and saucer was brought by Molly and Dominie poured Rohan's tea, aware of his eyes on her as she did so. But she felt sure his gaze was mechanical, that she might not have been there for all the real interest he took in her. She looked at him as she passed him his tea; he inclined his head and said a quiet, 'Thank you,' as he took the cup from her. He and Jake talked and Dominie was given the opportunity of examining his features more closely. Handsome he undoubtedly was, with that sort of attraction which could not fail to affect any woman with an ounce of romance in her, be she young or old. His skin was clear and very brown from the sun; his hair was thick and healthy, his brows straight, aristocratic, his teeth were white and even ... in fact, thought Dominie as she continued to stare, he was perfection itself. But there was about him something which seemed to offset the attractiveness of his features. There was a cynicism which jarred, and a certain ruthlessness lay half-hidden in those amber eyes. The mouth, sensuous and wide, portrayed a hardness, somehow, she decided; and that jawline ... It told its own story of the man's inflexibility.

It was inevitable that he should at last become aware of her keen interest and before she could lower her head she received an arrogant and questioning glance from him. A flush spread and she swallowed, averting her head, angry with herself for her interest. The man was probably filled with vanity as it was, without her flattering his ego by staring at him like a wide-eyed schoolgirl who had just found herself face to face with her favourite hero of the films.

To her surprise he spoke to her as he was leaving.

'Are you enjoying your enforced stay on our island, Miss Worthing?'

'Very much, thank you. Jake is a most charming host.' She stopped, not having meant to say anything like that. Her eyes flew to Jake, who was at that moment giving a little shrug, as if silently saying it was nothing. Rohan's eyes wandered from Dominie to Jake, a most odd expression in their depths. At that moment Molly appeared, informing Jake that he was wanted on the telephone and he rose, excusing himself, and went off towards the house.

'Jake appears to have developed a fatherly affection for you,' remarked Rohan unexpectedly, his gaze on Jake's broad back. At the sarcasm in his tone Dominie's chin lifted.

'I hadn't noticed,' she replied coldly.

His eyes widened; they seemed to scorch her.

'I'll bid you good afternoon, Miss Worthing,' he said crisply, and left her sitting at the table, her eyes following his tall figure as he strode with swift and easy grace across the lawn towards the drive along which he had come just half an hour earlier.

CHAPTER THREE

IN spite of her assertion that she would be able to find something suitable to wear Dominie felt rather drab as she emerged from her beautiful pink and white bedroom and moved towards the drawing-room in which some of the guests were already having drinks with Jake. The dress she wore was several sizes too large, and she had drawn it in with a beaded belt she had found. It was a peculiar shade of russet-red and seemed to accentuate the pallor of her skin, a pallor that had been increased within the last hour on her hearing the news from Jake that he'd had word that the ship was not now going to Madeira, as there had been a shortage of water on board and the ship was now speeding to Port Everglades, where a fresh supply could be obtained. Jake, all apologies and anxiety, had soothingly told her to forget the cruise altogether and remain on St Thomas as his guest until it was time to return to Southampton, where she could board the ship and take off her luggage. He had already been in contact with the ship, of course, and her luggage was quite safe, the cabin having been locked up by the steward when it was known that Dominie had missed the ship at St Thomas. Dominie agreed to forget the cruise, and although she was not unhappy at the prospect of staying at Sunset Lodge—just the reverse, in fact—she did seem to have a heaviness hanging about her, as if some trouble, or disaster, would ensue from her prolonging the visit. It was absurd, she knew, and yet, try as she would, she was quite unable to shake the feeling off.

Rohan was standing by the open french window when she entered the drawing-room. With him was a girl of about twenty-one, very slim and attractive, with slanting eyes and full red lips. Her skin was dark and Dominie formed the impression that she was part Spanish. But it transpired that the colour of her skin was merely the result of the sun. She was the daughter of wealthy parents and had nothing to do but sit about in the sun, Jake was later to inform Dominie.

At first, Dominie was so struck by the arresting couple standing there in the window, chatting in an intimate sort of way, that she saw no one else, but when presently she did look about her she gave a little gasp of horror. She was the only woman present who was not wearing a long dress. Hers was formal enough, but only calf-length. Colour mounting, she would have backed from the room, but Jake, apparently oblivious to anything being amiss with her attire, came swiftly forward and took her hand. She was introduced to several people, and all the women looked at her dress. Sylvia actually gave a small giggle as after the introduction Jake led Dominie off to someone else. Hearing this laugh, Dominie said, almost in tears,

'Jake, I don't want to stay. Will you say I'm off-colour, and let me leave?'

'Leave? Whatever for?' He stared at her, saw her blinking rapidly and frowned anxiously at her. 'My dear, you're crying!'

'Not quite. I'm wearing the wrong clothes. I didn't expect them all to be in long dresses.'

'What does it matter? You look very pretty——'

'No, Jake, I do not look pretty. This colour doesn't suit me because I'm far too pale. Added to this is the fact that the dress isn't suitable to the occasion, any-way——' She broke off as a young man approached.

'Jake, my turn next. May I meet your shipboard companion? I've heard all about her from Rohan.'

A frown caught Jake's brow. He made the intro-duction swiftly and once more led Dominie away, so they could whisper together.

'You should have let me buy you a dress. After all, it's entirely my fault that you're here.' Dominie said nothing, but merely glanced at the door as if she would immediately make her escape. 'It is, my dear,' Jake continued. 'I'm entirely to blame for the situa-tion you're in.' He glanced at her. '*I* think you look nice, and that's all that matters.' Affectionately he tucked his arm into hers. 'Come, let me give you a drink.'

'But——'

'You can't disappear now, Dominie.'

'You mean, it will embarrass you?'

'No, Dominie, but it will embarrass you—when you meet these people again.'

'They'd know why I went off?' she said, then in-stantly added, 'I shan't ever meet them again.'

'You will. Rohan is taking the Fortescues out to dinner on Thursday, and just a moment ago I heard him inviting one or two more people——'

'What has this got to do with me? I'm not invited.'

'But you are, Dominie. He's asked me to his dinner-party, and I'm to bring you too. I hope you'll come.'

This information left Dominie a trifle stunned, as she knew instinctively that Rohan did not like her. After a few seconds' deliberation, though, she realized that the invitation must include Jake's guest, since it was hardly conceivable that Jake would leave her behind.

After a few minutes the amused interest in her clothes faded and Dominie's embarrassment died with it. She was knowledgeable and intelligent and, therefore, able to hold her own in any conversation into which she was drawn. Jake was never very far away; he looked after her with the food and drink, taking her over to the buffet himself, and carrying her plate back to the seats, which were spread about the gardens, under trees or by exotic flowering bushes. An illuminated fountain added light to that given off by lamps in the trees and bright lights from the house. It was like fairyland, with the gentle trade-winds breeze cooling the evening air and spreading perfume from the flowers, so that it filled the entire garden.

'Happier now, Dominie?' asked Jake as he took his place beside her on the low cane garden seat.

'Yes, thank you, Jake.' She stopped as a couple came to join them, and automatically brought forward a chair which was by her side. The woman sat down on this, while her husband managed to find room on the seat by Jake.

'I see Rohan has found himself a young lady at last.' The woman, grey-haired and immaculately dressed, spoke conversationally to Jake, who sent Dominie a glance that clearly told her he had listened to Mrs Cookson's gossip before.

'I shouldn't imagine she could be described as his young lady,' Jake returned, looking over to where the striking couple stood, by the fountain. 'Rohan's never mentioned her to me, so he can't be all that friendly with her.'

'Oh, but you're wrong, Jake! He's been seen with her in London. He went over a couple of months ago, if you remember? The Fortescues were there and Rohan took Sylvia out every night—so we've been told. Also, he's stayed with them at their home in New York, and he and Sylvia were always together. Perhaps he's changed his mind about women,' she added, with a laugh which brought out all the hidden wrinkles at the sides of her eyes.

'I'd like to see him settled,' from her husband in slow and rather gruff tones. 'He had a bad time when he lost his sister. We all thought he'd never get over it.' He turned to Dominie. 'Lost her in an accident over in England,' he went on to explain. 'Some woman, drunk as a lord, caused the accident in which his sister was killed. He came back here broken. You can't imagine a man like Rohan being struck down with grief, can you?'

'No, not really.'

'He was. You know that, don't you, Jake?'

'Yes. And I'm sure he hasn't really got over it yet.'

'If it had happened to me I should be filled with bitterness that the woman got away with it,' interposed Mrs Cookson. 'It's dreadful to think that she caused a young girl's death and yet herself escaped. Were I in Rohan's place I'd be wishing I'd run into the

43

woman's car instead of trying to avoid it.'

'You don't know the circumstances, dear,' her husband said mildly. 'I'm always telling you not to be so quick to judge. Perhaps there was some excuse for her taking the drink.'

'Is there any excuse for being drunk in charge of a car?'

'None at all,' asserted Jake firmly. 'The woman ought to have been jailed!'

'She probably would have been, had they known who she was. Just drove away,' added Mr Cookson for Dominie's benefit, at which Jake intervened to inform him that Dominie had already heard all about the affair from him. 'Sorry, then,' said Mr Cookson. 'I hate to be a bore by repeating what people already know.'

His wife brought the conversation back to the girl who was with Rohan.

'Sylvia's a charming child—so unsophisticated and natural. They make a most impressive and handsome pair, don't you think?'

'Yes—yes, they do,' replied Dominie on realizing the question had been put to her. She did not consider the girl particularly unsophisticated, but naturally kept this to herself. Sylvia appeared—to Dominie, that was—to be a most assured and polished young lady ... and more than a little artificial, both in her make-up and in the amount of jewellery she wore. Nevertheless, Dominie could not deny that she was a most striking girl, and obviously the kind a man like Rohan de Arden would choose for a wife, should he ever decide to marry.

'There's the band starting up.' Mrs Cookson smiled at her husband. 'Arthur, will you dance with me?'

'Certainly, dear,' he returned obligingly, and led his

wife off in the direction of the room from which the music had come.

'Are you ready to dance, Dominie?'

She turned to Jake, who was already getting up.

'Do you mind if I sit here for a while? I like the quiet, and the cool breeze on my face.'

'Then stay by all means. You don't mind if I leave you? I must do my duty by the ladies.'

She smiled up at him.

'I don't mind in the least. I'll come inside in a little while.'

She sat for a time, then got up and strolled about the grounds, trying to name the plants. The tree over there was a frangipani, she knew that because Susie had told her. And that hedge was made up of a mixture of pink oleanders and hibiscus ... She had wandered from the lights and the trees became shadows in the violet haze of night. The moon was a mere crescent, the stars lost in fleecy white cloud. How still; how quiet, with the strains of the steel band becoming fainter and fainter. Voices! Dominie stopped and leant against the trunk of a tree.

'But you kept looking at her!'

'Imagination, my dear Sylvia.'

'I saw you!' The voice was petulant but so very attractive. Dominie suddenly knew that Sylvia was clever as well as beautiful. 'You're trying to make me jealous, and—and I hate you!'

A small amused laugh and then,

'Tears, my lovely child? Don't be silly. I look at no one but you.'

'I think you're a philanderer, and I've decided I don't want anything more to do with you!'

'Throwing me over? And all because you imagine—

imagine,' he repeated with emphasis, 'that I looked at Jake's little friend?'

Dominie gave a start. She would never have imagined it was she about whom Sylvia was talking.

'Throwing you over! I've never been your girl-friend, Rohan!'

A frown touched Dominie's wide brow. What was the girl up to? The couple had stopped walking and Dominie pressed against the tree, thankful now that her dress was dark.

'Who,' said Rohan, ignoring that last angry statement from Sylvia, 'would want to look at a little mouse like Miss Worthing?'

A giggle followed swiftly on this and Dominie squirmed.

'She is funny, isn't she? Fancy coming to the party in a dress like that. I just gasped at the little dowd, and couldn't believe my eyes. Who is she, anyway?'

'Someone Jake took pity on aboard the ship. You know what Jake is where women are concerned?'

'No, I don't. You've spoken about him once or twice, but I haven't taken much notice.'

'He's soft with them. Admits he's afraid of hurting them. I expect the little Worthing was lonely and so he decided to father her.'

'Father? Is that all? There's nothing more in it?'

'I shouldn't think so. She's supposed to be leaving here next week—Friday, I think.'

Quivering hands went to Dominie's hot cheeks; her temper was as high as it could be. Nothing would have given her greater satisfaction than to confront the pair and let them know she had overheard what they had to say about her. But she held her fury in check, because of Jake and his friendship for the man. So differ-

46

ent they were. It seemed impossible that Jake could like a man so insufferable as Rohan de Arden.

'Kiss me, Rohan,' came the aching request quite suddenly.

'Glad to oblige, my love...' The silence following this lasted a long time, and Dominie would have done anything to be able to escape unseen. She had to remain where she was, though, pressed against the tree. 'Are you still determined to give me up?'

'I haven't decided,' purringly—like a pretty kitten, fluffy and white and very cuddly. 'I can have my pick, you know.'

'Undoubtedly.' The tones were smooth, unemotional. Dominie was exceedingly puzzled by the relationship existing between these two. She had a dawning suspicion that each was playing with the other, but she could not yet gather whether it was marriage to which they were trying to lead one another.

'You see, Rohan, I'm not in love with you.'

'No?' Silence. Dominie had the impression that Rohan was stifling a yawn. 'Then how come you to be jealous of the little Worthing?'

Dominie's teeth gritted together.

'I wasn't jealous——'

'You said you were.'

'I said you were trying to make me jealous!'

'I stand corrected.' Another silence. 'Come, my child, we shall be missed and people will think things. You wouldn't like that, would you?'

'Indeed no! I quite forgot your reputation. People will *naturally* think things.'

'My reputation?' The low rich voice was edged with interest all at once. 'Tell me about it. What sort of a

47

reputation do I have?'

'You know very well. Up till now you've wanted women only for one thing.'

'I have? What thing?'

'Rohan, don't put on this pretence! If you've been seen with a woman, then it's been assumed she's your mistress.'

'And how many women have I been seen with, might I ask?'

'There was one called Freda.'

'I believe there was. She wanted to marry me, if my memory's not at fault.' Humour fringed his tones; Dominie could almost see those sensuous lips twitching out there, in the darkness of the night.

'But you seduced her instead.'

'She wanted to be seduced,' was Rohan's cool response, and Sylvia uttered a disgusted little gasp.

'Men are sickening! I think I shall be an old maid.'

'They're referred to as bachelor girls today.'

'I hate you!'

'How many other women have I been seen with?' inquired Rohan, bypassing this vehement assertion.

'I seem to have heard of one called Joan.'

'Beautiful but dumb, as the saying goes. Yes, I do remember her. She also had marriage in mind.'

'Did you seduce her too?'

'I believe I did.'

'Shameful conduct! Shameless man! No, I shall not have anything more to do with you! We're finished!'

'I'm distracted. For several months I've given you all my attention and now you're throwing me over. I hope you'll never regret it, Sylvia.'

A very strange light entered Dominie's eyes. Yes, she felt she had the whole situation quite sorted out...

'Have I hurt you—really?' Soft tones denoting a sort of fragility. And a small catch rather like a sigh of contrition. Which one of them would win this little game? wondered Dominie, who could have been exceedingly amused were it not for the sting she herself had received on hearing the disparaging remarks these two had made about her.

'Really. I shall take you back now, and leave you. I'll spend the rest of the evening drinking.'

'Oh, Rohan, forgive me! It's j-just that I'm frightened.'

'Of what, you ridiculous child?'

'Of you! And of myself as well. I like you no end, and don't want to hurt you. But as I'm not in love with you I'm afraid of myself. I might make a mistake because of my pity.'

'You mean,' said Rohan on a most odd note which Dominie could never have interpreted, 'that if I asked you to marry me you might accept—out of pity?'

'Yes, that's right. But don't ask me to marry you— please, dearest Rohan!'

A deep sigh came over the night air.

'I can wait, my love ... until you know your own mind.'

The two strolled on and became shadows as they skirted the brightly-lit lawns and took the path round the side of the house, from where they would enter the room in which the band was playing.

Sylvia was a smart girl, but Rohan was no fool. He knew what Sylvia's game was; of this Dominie was fully convinced, while Sylvia had no idea that Rohan was indulging in a game also. The girl had marriage in mind; the man was bent on seduction.

Thinking about it for a long while after she had slid

between the clean cool sheets, Dominie decided that the result could very well be stalemate.

Determined not to appear as a 'little mouse' next time, Dominie asked Jake to drive her into Charlotte Amalie, as she wished to buy an evening gown.

'Let me pay for it?' he begged as he parked the car at the back of Veterans Drive. 'It would make me happy to do so.'

But Dominie shook her head.

'I've left most of my money at the Purser's Office on the ship,' she said, 'but I have enough to buy a dress.'

'You're a most independent girl,' he sighed, but took her arm and led her across the car park and along the road to where a shady little alleyway, with seats set out under the palms, led to the shopping centre.

'Does this alley have a name?' asked Dominie, enchanted with it.

'Yes, it's called Hibiscus Alley—— No, it isn't; that's the next one. This is Jasmine Lane.'

'It's fascinating! Are there any more?'

'Orchid Row. They're really part of the shopping area, as you can see——' Jake gestured towards the brightly-lit shops lining the alley. 'The whole is called Beretta Centre, and it's said to be the most attractive shopping area in the whole of the Caribbean. You can buy anything from expensive jewellery and perfume to glass and china and leatherwork—everything you can possibly think of. If you want a reasonably-priced dress I'll show you where to go; if you want a high fashion creation from Contessa Bernardini then you must go to The Spanish Main.'

'The Spanish Main? Is that a place to buy clothes?' Jake merely nodded in answer to her question and some strange tingling of anxiety possessed her even before he said, a few moments later,

'Let me buy you a dress, Dominie—a really beautiful one.'

She shook her head swiftly.

'It's kind of you, Jake, but I must buy my own.'

'Very well,' resignedly but with a small sigh which plainly told her that to buy her a dress would afford him exceeding pleasure.

They entered several shops, but Dominie saw nothing she liked and she could not help thinking of the pretty clothes she had left on the ship. Suddenly they were looking in a window where no fewer than three lovely evening gowns caught her eye.

'These are what I was telling you about. You'll find them very expensive.' Jake was ready to walk on, surmising that she would not be interested. In the ordinary way she would have looked, admired, and gone off to find something more suited to her pocket. But stabbing at her consciousness were Rohan de Arden's words, 'Who would look at a little mouse like Miss Worthing?' and also Sylvia's amused giggle and her response, 'She is funny, isn't she? Fancy coming to the party in a dress like that. I just gasped at the little dowd...'

Dominie had never before been called a dowd. She was pretty, to say the least; this she knew without being immodest. True, she could not compete with the exotic beauty of Sylvia who in any case was six years younger than she, and who, never having known poverty or sorrow, looked even younger than her years. But although she could not compete in looks with the girl she could at least be as beautifully gowned.

'We'll go in,' she decided, and, concealing his

51

surprise, Jake followed her into the shop. She had forty pounds in her purse; the dress was one hundred and fifty dollars. Ridiculous even to think of it, she chided herself, and turned to Jake before she had time to allow her common sense to override her desire. 'Would you lend me the rest? I'll send it on to you immediately I get home.'

'I'll give it to you—— Please, my dear. You look so ravishing in it. Let me pay the difference.'

'I'll just borrow it, Jake,' she returned gently, and once again he gave a little sigh. 'And now for my hair,' she was saying presently. 'Can you tell me the best place?—and—er—lend me a little more money?' What had come over her? She was being utterly shameless, asking for these loans from a man she had known less than a fortnight. But she was determined to show those two arrogant creatures! They would eat their words when she appeared at the dinner-party in her expensive gown, with her hair done by Charlotte Amalie's most exclusive hairdresser. 'Do you think I'll be able to make an appointment—or will they be booked up?'

'We can but try, my dear.' Jake smiled affectionately at her. 'You're going to stun them all!'

That, she told herself, was her intention! Those two particularly, though. She would be proud, too, and even haughty with Rohan, should he deign to speak to her, as surely he must, seeing that she was his guest.

The dinner was at the Virgin Isle Hilton, where one corner of the Frangi-Pani dining-room was reserved for Rohan and his guests. These included the Osbornes, a young couple who owned a chain of boutiques in the Virgin Islands, the Meads, an elderly couple who were retired and lived about a mile from Rohan and, of course, the Fortescues.

Dominie arrived with Jake, who an hour before had just stood and stared at her, almost speechless with admiration. She would be the most beautiful and elegant lady there, he had at last declared, when he had managed to find his tongue.

A waiter appeared and conducted them to the Foolish Virgin Bar where all but the Meads were already gathered for drinks. Rohan was the first to see them; he smiled at Jake before his eyes moved to Dominie ... and then he seemed to catch his breath, and the smile faded for one amazed second before, recovering, he said graciously, striding towards them from his place at the bar,

'What a charming companion you have, Jake.'

Dominie's head was held high, but at this she inclined it slightly and said with faint hauteur,

'Thank you, Mr de Arden,' and she saw his amber eyes flicker, and move from her face to her hair, beautifully coiffured, and then his eyes swept downwards, the full length of her dress. It was of heavy white satin trimmed with hundreds of tiny coloured beads on the collar and hem. The mandarin collar was all that held up the front; her shoulders and back, flawless and tanned to a rich golden brown, were bare. The toe-length skirt was slit at one side to well above the knee. It was the most glamorous gown Dominie had ever owned and on getting it home after buying it she had suffered an hour or two of sheer agony at her extravagance as she dwelt on the cost for one evening only, as it was most unlikely she would ever wear it again.

But as she noted the effect of Rohan and that on Sylvia, who was staring, dumbfounded, from where she

53

stood, some distance away, with her parents, Dominie felt that her dress had been worth every penny it had cost.

'Come and have a drink.' Rohan's voice, rich and low and possessing the merest hint of an American drawl, cut into the small silence following Dominie's coolly-spoken words and she and Jake moved over to where the others were standing, chatting over their drinks. All eyes became focused on Dominie; she dominated the scene entirely and elation rose within her. She could hold her own in this distinguished and fashionable gathering. Mrs Fortescue's glance went from Dominie to her daughter and she frowned slightly. Comparing, mused Dominie with a secret smile. The girl's eyes were still fixed disbelievingly on Dominie, and she also frowned. She was immaculate and there was an innate confidence about her which Dominie lacked, but she was no longer the main centre of attraction.

'Miss Worthing, what are you having...?'

Dominie scarcely heard Rohan, for Grace Osborne was actually commenting on the dress.

'It's delicious,' she added with a tinge of envy. 'Where on earth did you get it, Miss Worthing? Did you bring it with you?'

'I bought it in Charlotte Amalie——'

'Then why didn't I see it first!'

'Wouldn't fit you, darling,' interposed her husband with a grin. 'I'm always telling you you eat too much.'

'Abominable man! Why did I marry you!'

'For my money, I shouldn't wonder,' was the swift reply, and everyone laughed.

'Frank Osborne's a millionaire,' whispered Jake a moment later as he and Dominie sipped their drinks.

54

'I should imagine this island's full of millionaires.'

'It's certainly a very wealthy island. The rich come to the Caribbean to build magnificent homes in the sun. You should see the Osbornes' place—it's a dream, a veritable palace.'

'And Rohan's? Is that also a palace?'

'Indeed it is, but in a smaller way. The Osbornes' place is enormous; Rohan, who's probably even more wealthy than they, doesn't flaunt his money as Frank does.'

'I'm surprised——' Dominie broke off, the words having escaped involuntarily.

'You don't like Rohan?' from Jake in a curious tone as his eyes went to the man under discussion. Rohan was by far the most distinguished-looking man present in the bar. His evening clothes were of superlative cut and quality, and he possessed the kind of physique that was bound to show them off to perfection.

'I haven't had much opportunity of forming an opinion,' she evaded, her mind on that conversation she had overheard between Rohan and his beautiful companion. Dominie more than disliked the man: she detested him!

'He's the most genuine man I know,' stated Jake in his thoughtful way. 'I'd trust him with my life. I know he appears off-hand with most women, but as I told you, he has cause to dislike them. If he marries Sylvia I shall be most surprised, since he's always struck me as favouring bachelordom—this even when he was keeping company with Nina. I was never quite as certain as all the others that he would decide to marry her.'

'You weren't?'

Jake shook his head, his eyes wandering as the Meads entered the bar. Both seemed to blink questioningly on seeing Dominie, as if for the moment wondering who she was. With recognition came admiring looks, and Mrs Mead whispered something to her husband.

'I used sometimes to think the affair would peter out,' Jake was saying, his gaze now on Rohan. 'Yes ... even if Nina had not transferred her affections to someone else I rather think that Rohan would in the end have himself ended the affair.'

'It must have been a blow to his pride—Nina giving him up.' Dominie stopped rather abruptly, sorry she had said a thing like that to Jake, who was such a good friend of Rohan. Jake merely shrugged and made no comment.

'It looks as if we're to go in to dinner,' remarked Frank, who had come to join them, thus terminating the conversation about Rohan. 'Are you enjoying your stay on our island?' he added with a smile for Dominie, who nodded instantly.

'I'm having a wonderful time. Jake's been taking me round in his car. The views and the countryside are superb.'

Frank's smile broadened.

'And I suppose you've been to the Mountain Top Restaurant and drunk their famous Banana Daiquiri? —and sat on Drake's seat and made a wish?'

Dominie laughed.

'Yes, I've done those things, and many more. I've seen the limbo dancers and the steel bands and listened to the calypso singers at the beach club down in the bay there.'

'So you've a lot to tell your people and friends when you get back to England?'

She nodded but made no reply. Taking her arm,

Jake escorted her into the Frangi-Pani room and to their table which was shaded by potted palms, and very dimly lighted from candles and muted wall-lamps.

'Have you no relatives at all?' he asked when they were seated.

'Just an aged aunt—if she's still living. I haven't heard from her for years. My last two letters went unanswered, so I haven't bothered any more. She's very distant—not a blood relation even.'

'Sad. It must be a lonely sort of feeling when you have no one at all of your own.'

'It is. When I had Jerry it didn't seem to matter that I'd no one else. I had long since become used to the fact of having no parents, and so long as I had Jerry I was happy.'

Jake nodded thoughtfully. His good-natured face was clouded and his voice was gentle when he spoke.

'I think I understand, my dear. And I think it's the same with Rohan. He loved his sister dearly, and as he was her guardian he also had the protective instinct one would expect in those circumstances. I believe he's still missing her; and I sometimes think, too, that he blames himself for her death. He once said he should never have allowed her to go to England and become an actress. Had she not been in your country the accident would never have happened, you see.'

'Yes...' A small pause as Dominie's eyes strayed. Rohan was talking to Sylvia, his dark head bent, and very close to hers. 'He was not strict with his sister, apparently. This surprises me, as he appears to be a stern sort of man.' She was noticing his mouth and jaw, and taking in the inflexibility she saw there.

'He was strict, in many ways, but I expect he felt unwilling to curb her when it came to her career. She was extremely talented and acting was what she wanted. As I've said, he later regretted allowing her to have her own way.'

'Perhaps she would have insisted, though.'

'No doubt of it, as I told him when he spoke of this self-blame. She would most certainly have defied him once she was free of his authority.'

'But of course the accident wouldn't have happened, because she wouldn't have been in that particular place at that particular time.'

'True, but I believe in fate, Dominie.'

She felt tears prick her eyes suddenly.

'Then fate is cruel. My brother was only eighteen, and for all I say it myself, he was one of the good people of this world. Jerry never said an unkind word to anyone in the whole of his life.'

The band was playing; Rohan and Sylvia had got up to dance and in order to put an end to a painful subject Jake asked Dominie to dance. The second course was served when they sat down again. Immediately it was eaten Rohan came to Dominie, inviting her to dance. She slid into his arms, suddenly tensed for no reason she could explain. She said, when they were at the other side of the room,

'May I take this opportunity of thanking you for inviting me this evening? I'm enjoying it immensely.' Her voice was one of cool politeness and Rohan leant away from her for a second, appearing to be a trifle puzzled by her manner. She wondered whether he would be put out were she to tell him that she had overheard his conversation with Sylvia.

'It's a pleasure to have you, Miss Worthing. I'm glad that you've stayed long enough to come.'

'I'm not leaving until Tuesday,' she informed him,

just for something to say.

'I thought it was tomorrow you were leaving?'

'Didn't Jake tell you of the altered plans? The ship's on its way to Florida, and then it's making for home.'

'No, Jake never mentioned this. So you're not bothering to rejoin it?'

'No. Jake asked me to stay with him and as I'm enjoying myself there didn't seem to be any reason for leaving. I shall fly straight back to England and pick up my belongings in Southampton.' Her tones were still cool, but not quite as cool as she would have liked them to be. For she was, to her astonishment, strangely affected by the nearness of the man, by his touch and his voice and the superb rhythm of his body as he danced. When he took her back to the table her glance caught that of Sylvia. The girl's eyes were narrowed, her lovely mouth petulant. Deliberately she turned her head away from Rohan as he sat down.

Dutifully Rohan danced with all his women guests, but to Dominie's astonishment she herself was more favoured even than the lovely Sylvia.

'I must congratulate you on your dancing,' he remarked on one occasion. 'You do a great deal of it at home?'

'I scarcely ever go out.' She would have bitten back the words if she could, as they revealed her lack of social life.

Rohan made no comment on this; they were now outside, dancing to the steel band, and he gradually edged from the floor to the side and Dominie found herself standing alone with him, gazing across the sea to where a ship was anchored, its brilliant lights shimmering on the soft dark waters of the Caribbean. Water island drowsed in the distance while behind

59

them, as Dominie swung right round to take in the full vista, rose the lush tree-clad mountains.

'It's all so incredibly beautiful,' she breathed, half forgetting her companion, standing there, silent and thoughtful. 'Wherever one goes one has a view of other islands. How many are there?'

'You mean the Virgins?' She nodded and was told there were about fifty belonging to the U.S. and thirty owned by Britain.

'So many!'

'Not all are inhabited, as you probably know. Of the U.S. Virgins only three are of any major importance.'

'Have you always lived here, Mr de Arden?'

'My parents had a house here when they were young, and we used to spend a good deal of our time on the island.' Rohan paused, and a frown touched his brow. Watching him, Dominie guessed that his thoughts had run on to less happy times—when his father went off with that young girl. 'I myself settled here just over ten years ago,' he added at length, then abruptly changed the subject, pointing out a few islands and giving her the names of them.

'We can see a similar view to this from Jake's terrace —but of course you know,' she said, flushing slightly. And then she added, 'I expect you have the same view? Can you see Magens Bay and St John, and the British Virgins—some of them, I mean?'

Rohan nodded his head, glancing down at her and suddenly saying,

'You must see my place before you leave. I'll tell Jake to bring you to dinner tomorrow evening.'

'That's very kind, Mr de Arden.' She felt shy all at once, because of his interest and the dropping of his mask of austerity which seemed always to be there even when he was chatting with his friends.

'Not at all, Miss Worthing; I shall enjoy the pleasure of your company.'

She stared at him. Was he sincere? Something like a warning seemed to stab at her subconscious. Her uneasiness increased when he took her arm, cupping her elbow in his hand, and guided her back to where Sylvia was sitting with her parents, watching the dark-skinned men on the steel drums. The action was even more unexpected than his invitation, but for the present she had no time to dwell on it, her attention diverted by the expression on Sylvia's face. Her mouth was tight with anger, yet it trembled slightly; her eyes glittered as they met those of Dominie, then seemed, astonishingly, to fill up with tears. She lowered her head before Rohan should notice, and shortly afterwards, when he was dancing with the girl, Dominie saw that neither spoke to one another.

'There's to be a fashion show.' Jake spoke into Dominie's ear. 'They have men's fashions as well as women's. You should enjoy it.'

After the show came the limbo dancing, then the band continued to play for the guests to dance again. All took place out in the open air, amidst a setting of fairy-tale colour provided by the tropical trees and shrubs, by the table lights—candles burning in coloured jars—and by the costumes of the steel band players. The air was filled with heady, exotic smells; the gentle cooling trade-winds blew in from the northeast, swaying the coconut palms and the lovely flamboyant trees.

At last the party broke up and Dominie found herself beside Jake in the car. They crossed the island to the Atlantic side, skirting St Peter Mountain and coming into sight of the beautiful Magens Bay, far down below.

'I must congratulate you on capturing the attention of Rohan,' Jake said with a laugh as he brought the car to a halt outside the house. 'The pretty Sylvia appeared to be more than a little troubled by his very marked interest in you.'

Dominie was getting out of the car; she was glad of the dimness, for a flush had risen swiftly on the utterance of her companion's words.

'It was only the dress,' she murmured in response as Jake came round from his side and joined her. 'He didn't even notice me the other evening.'

'You look lovely, apart from the dress,' he said, and stood staring down at her. 'Yes, very lovely indeed.'

His words remained with her for a long while and she could not sleep. It had been an exciting experience, being there among that wealthy throng. It was another world from that to which she was used, a totally unreal world for all except those who lived permanently in it.

But the most exciting experience of all for Dominie was in fact capturing the attention of the most attractive and distinguished man present...

CHAPTER FOUR

LIFTING a hand in response as the children waved to her, Dominie watched them race across the lawn and disappear into the palm-shaded avenue at the other end of which was the pool where Jake was taking his customary afternoon swim.

Reluctantly she allowed her eyes to wander to the nearby small rise, clothed with tamarind trees and scarlet oleanders. The rise was really part of Rohan's land, although not in his gardens proper. Beyond the rise stood his house, hidden from Dominie's pensive gaze but clearly outlined in her mind. Windward Crest ... The most tastefully-designed house she had ever seen; the decor too was breathtakingly beautiful, yet simple, somehow, revealing its owner's abhorrence of ostentation and unnecessary show. The grounds had, in Jake's words, 'cost the earth' to landscape, yet they also possessed a simplicity that revealed good taste rather than grandeur. There were the usual kaleidoscopes of exotic trees and shrubs, the entrancing tropical flowers cascading over trellises and walls, their fragrance pervading the air to tantalize the senses and to bring to mind such lovely-sounding words as hibiscus and poinsettia, allamanda and bougainvillaea. But although Rohan's gardens boasted every tree, and most of the flowers, which grew and flourished in the Caribbean, the whole was so arranged that one had to roam about in order to discover much of the beauty. With other gardens Dominie had seen the whole colourscape was revealed at a glance, dazzling and a trifle overpowering.

Dominie, standing on the terrace, stiffened suddenly and withdrew her gaze. Rohan had appeared and was standing at the foot of the rise, staring down to the azure lagoon far below.

Colour flooded her face and once again she wondered how she had come to accept Jake's offer of the post of nanny to his children. His offer had come on the day of her departure; he had asked her to return and care for Susie and Geoffrey. His offer was tempting in itself, but Dominie had at once admitted that it was Rohan's face, rising up before her, that had been the deciding factor when her decision was made. Many women must have fallen victim to his charms, she had told herself. Better escape now, for the man was far, far too attractive.

She was not quite sure when the impact of him first hit her; what she did know was that after that evening spent at his home, with his charm being in evidence the whole time, and his smile so often directed at her, she found herself in a sort of daze where nothing and no one seemed tangible except the man himself. Sylvia had been furious at his giving Dominie his attention, and so had her mother, but both appeared to have hidden it from him, for he never seemed to notice any sort of 'atmosphere'—or if he did, thought Dominie afterwards, he managed to keep his observations to himself.

Dominie felt awkward and shy, and even guilty. Never did she feel exultant because of his interest; she was far too puzzled by it. The following day Jake made another reference to it and smilingly added,

'You should be congratulating yourself, Dominie. With single women Rohan is notoriously polite but distant.'

'What about Sylvia?' she had instantly countered, more in order to conceal her own feelings than anything else. 'He isn't distant with her.'

'True, and it would seem that he's interested in her. But never before has Rohan been known to give his interest to two women at once. In fact, during the five years since the break with Nina he's had the odd affair —matter of convenience,' Jake added with a grin, 'and that's about all.'

Allowing her eyes to stray to the rise again, Dominie found that Rohan had gone. She swallowed hard, releasing the hurtful pressure in her throat. What a fool she had been to accept Jake's offer ... simply because she could not bear the thought of never setting eyes on Rohan again. He liked her, she concluded, and although she retained no conscious thoughts of competing with the beautiful Sylvia, there most certainly was in her innermost mind the merest germ of hope. He liked her, she had told herself again, for otherwise why should he give her his attention?

It was only after she had returned to Sunset Lodge and settled in that Dominie discovered that Rohan had been using her to make Sylvia jealous.

The information had come from Mrs Fortescue who, with her husband and Sylvia, were making another visit to the island, having gone home about the same time as Dominie had left for England. This visit was a flying one and, somehow, Dominie gained the impression that Mrs Fortescue had engineered it for the specific purpose of talking to Dominie. She knew of her return and the post she had taken with Jake, for Rohan had been over to New York and stayed with the Fortescues just a week after Dominie had returned to the island, having rented the whole house to Mavis and James until the time when they should find a place to buy, which was their intention.

Mrs Fortescue had come over on her own to Sunset Lodge, and she was fortunate enough to catch Dominie alone, the children being at school and Jake's having gone into Charlotte Amalie to do some shopping. Dominie was in the garden, cutting flowers for the house, and she glanced up in surprise as Mrs Fortescue came towards her.

'Ah, Miss Worthing,' she began effusively, 'I'm glad I've found an opportunity of seeing you alone.' She stopped then, appearing to have difficulty in framing her words. A slight shrug portrayed the fact of her having decided there was no delicate way in which the matter could be broached and she said, 'It's about Rohan, and the attention he gave you on one or two occasions. He's desperately in love with my daughter, as everyone knows, and she's in love with him. But Rohan doesn't know this, as she's playing around—you know what young girls are these days?' She paused for some comment, but Dominie was speechless with surprise, and in addition she knew a rising indignation at the woman's implication that she herself was not of Sylvia's generation. 'The consequence is that Rohan's been using you to make my daughter jealous, and now that you've returned it's conceivable that he'll continue to do so. I felt it incumbent on me to warn you, dear, for the man is so inordinately attractive and I don't want you to be hurt. So many women have fallen in love with him, and he has no real interest in them; Jake will tell you the same if you ask him.'

Crimson with anger, Dominie put down the basket of flowers and faced the woman.

'Mrs Fortescue,' she said icily, 'I would inform you that I have no designs whatsoever on the man your daughter hopes to marry——'

'Hopes? She can marry him just whenever she chooses!' The woman dropped her affectation of friendliness and charm, replacing it with a manner of arrogance and superiority. 'What I said to you was merely in the nature of a friendly warning. If you disregard it you'll be sorry!' The woman stood there, waiting for some response, but Dominie strode away and left her standing there, dark fury in her eyes as they followed the slender figure until it disappeared round the corner of the house.

Standing on the back patio now, Dominie dwelt on what the woman had said. And she knew for sure that Mrs Fortescue was right in her deductions: Rohan had used her, Dominie, in order to make Sylvia jealous. And he would continue to use her—if she allowed him to do so, which she definitely would not. There was to be a moonlight bathing party this evening over at his place and she was invited, but already she had decided not to put in an appearance. Jake would of course expect her to go with him, but loath as she was to disappoint him she would not place herself at the convenience of the despicable Rohan de Arden.

Her eyes narrowed suddenly as the man himself appeared, and she felt her body stiffen; she would have liked to escape, but it was too late, and she gestured with her hand, indicating a chair, which he accepted.

'Is Jake about?' he wanted to know, glancing sideways at the open window of Jake's study. 'Would you tell him I want to speak to him?'

'Of course. He's in the pool—or was, a few minutes ago.' She spoke with deliberate coldness, as she always had since the discovery of his using her for his own ends.

Rohan looked at her in a puzzled manner and said suddenly,

'Is something wrong, Miss Worthing? I can't help having the impression that I've done something to upset you.'

Under his keen regard Dominie sensed his wish to read her thoughts.

'I don't know how you can have gained an impression like that, Mr de Arden,' she returned with the same cold inflection to her voice. 'We scarcely know each other. How could you do something to upset me?'

Impatiently he sighed, and his mouth tightened a little. His amber eyes still searched and Dominie lowered hers. Rohan remained silent for a while, appearing to be interested in a hummingbird pivoting about among the flowers in the border close by.

'If Jake's in the pool then I had better go over to him,' he said at last, rising.

'Mr de Arden,' she said impulsively as he was about to move away, 'I won't be coming to the party tonight. I'm—er—tired these days, so I shall be going to bed early.'

Rohan, about to step off the patio on to the steps, turned and looked down into her flushed face. Already she wished she had held her tongue, had left her excuse to be conveyed by Jake, later, when he went to the party.

'You're—er—tired these days?' he echoed, distinct mockery in his tone. 'What sort of an excuse is that, might I ask?'

She stared, taken by surprise that he should be interested enough to go into the matter.

'The children...' she murmured, avoiding his gaze. His attractiveness was devastating; she was intensely affected by it, and depression swept through her. If only she had refused Jake's offer she would have forgotten the man by now. Instead, every meeting with him intensified his attraction for her.

'The children? You mean that you're overworked with them?' Scepticism edged his voice and was reflected in his eyes as they examined her face as if to find some signs of this tiredness she mentioned. 'Where are the children now?'

Her flush deepened as she told him they were in the pool with Jake.

'It's just that I don't feel like going tonight,' she added, speaking her thoughts aloud.

'So it isn't tiredness brought on by overwork?' His tones became curt and faintly accusing. 'Perhaps you'll give me the real reason for your last-minute change of mind about the party?'

'Does it matter?'

Rohan sent her a frowning glance.

'One usually has a reasonable excuse for turning down an invitation, especially one that has, in the first instance, been accepted. Dominie,' he added with abrupt deliberation, and bending his head slightly so that his face came closer to hers, 'I demand to know the reason for this change of mind.'

Dominie ... The name had rolled almost excitingly off his tongue, enriched by the hint of an American accent and the merest touch of a French one. This latter he had inherited from his father, Jake had said. Dominie suspected that those sensuous lips had also been a legacy from his father.

'I said I was tired,' she replied defensively, then took a backward step as she saw by the sudden flash of his eyes that his temper had risen.

'If I knew you better,' he snapped, 'I'd shake you, good and hard!'

Amazed, she just gaped at him. The aloof and superior Rohan de Arden speaking like this!

'I'm afraid, Mr de Arden, that I don't understand you.'

The amber eyes glinted, but Rohan made no answer or comment, and his customary cool composure was instantly resumed.

'Never mind,' he said curtly. 'If you'll excuse me I'll go and find Jake.'

Confused by his manner towards her, Dominie watched him as he strode towards the avenue of Royal Palms through which the children had recently vanished. What a striking figure he made, and what assurance! There was poise in every step he took, in the way he covered the distance with such grace and ease, in the manner in which his head was held, so proudly on those broad and arrogant shoulders. Why had he spoken to her like that? And for him to become angry ... it was baffling in the extreme, for she felt it could not have anything to do with his using her to make Sylvia jealous. In any case, the girl would not be present this evening, as she and her parents were not on the island.

Dominie swallowed hard. She wanted to go to the party, no doubt of that. She wanted to have a little of Rohan's attention, when Sylvia was not present ... But in all probability she would not have received any, since for Rohan there would be no profit in it, not with Sylvia being absent.

Would Sylvia marry him in the end? Dominie reflected on her own previous conclusions that both were playing a game with one another; she was still of the opinion that Rohan had seduction in mind rather than marriage, but on the other hand, Sylvia was clever. Also, Rohan must be greatly attracted to her, for otherwise he would not have gone to the lengths of using another girl in order to create jealousy. Perhaps, mused Dominie with a deep dejected sigh, Sylvia would win after all.

Jake was troubled on learning from Rohan that

Dominie was not intending to go to the party; he spoke of it immediately he and Rohan appeared. He had a beach coat draped on his shoulders and a towel in his hand. The children were hanging on to Rohan's hands, and chattering to him, and he was smiling down at them in turn. When his eyes met those of Dominie, however, the smile faded as his mouth tightened.

'Rohan tells me you're not coming to the party tonight. He says you're tired. Is this true? Are the children too much for you?'

Dominie went red, noting the satisfaction appearing in Rohan's eyes as she did so.

'Of course they're not,' she replied, sending Rohan a speaking glance. What must Jake be thinking? The children were at school all day, and at the week-ends Jake was invariably there to help entertain them. When there was shopping to do the four of them went together in the car; similarly when they went off to the beach they were all together. Dominie really had very little to do, and she had twice remarked on this to her employer, who passed it off, saying she was doing all that he expected of her. And now it must seem that she had been complaining, that she had given Rohan the impression that she was overworked. 'It's just that I don't want to go to the party.'

Rohan shrugged and spoke before Jake had time to do so.

'It's a woman's prerogative to change her mind,' he said casually. 'Don't let us press her, Jake.'

'But...' Jake tailed off, cut short by something in Dominie's expression. When Rohan had gone she confided in him, as she could find no other way of explaining her attitude.

'Mrs Fortescue said that?' he exclaimed when she had finished speaking. 'What a disgusting lack of delicacy and tact! How dared she?'

'She's anxious for her daughter to marry Rohan, that's obvious.'

'But to talk like that to you! Rohan would be furious if he knew.' Jake paused, frowning in thought. 'It isn't at all like Rohan to stoop to that sort of thing,' he mused at length. 'I'm not at all convinced that the wretched woman has her facts right.'

'She has, Jake. Why else should a man like Rohan give me any attention? He did—you remarked on it yourself, if you remember?'

'I'm not denying he gave you his attention. I felt, somehow, that he—well—liked you, rather.'

Dominie's lip trembled slightly.

'I thought the same,' she murmured, wondering what Jake would think were she to inform him that the attention Rohan had given her had in effect been responsible for her decision to accept the post Jake had offered to her.

Jake glanced swiftly at her.

'You thought he liked you...?' An awkward pause and then, 'In what way, Dominie?'

'Oh, just in a—a sort of—of impersonal way,' she replied airily, hoping to deflect his thoughts from the course they were quite plainly taking. 'I rather hoped we'd be—friends, or perhaps I should say, friendly acquaintances.'

Jake appeared relieved, for which Dominie was heartily thankful. It would add immeasurably to her humiliation were Jake ever to guess how she felt about his friend.

'I shouldn't take that woman's words to heart,' he

advised. 'Rohan's above using one woman in order to provoke another to jealousy. No, the idea's preposterous!' he added emphatically. 'If you knew him a little better you'd scoff at the notion.'

'Then why did he suddenly take an interest in me?' she asked, recalling with an inward squirm the conversation she had heard between Rohan and his girlfriend. 'I'm sure Rohan really considers me an uninteresting sort of person.'

Jake frowned again.

'Why on earth should you say that? No one could consider you uninteresting.'

Dominie hesitated, half inclined to tell Jake of what she had overheard, but she refrained, remembering in time that Rohan was a very great friend of his. Instead she said, forcing a laugh,

'You're prejudiced, Jake. You don't ever seem able to find a fault with me.'

'True,' he agreed, looking straight at her. He seemed to give a sigh, and he appeared quite old all at once. 'As far as I can see, my dear, you haven't any faults.'

'Everyone has faults. I'm sure I have dozens!'

Jake laughed and shook his head, but made no comment, changing the subject as he asked her to reconsider her decision about the party.

'I shan't enjoy it half as much if you're not there,' he told her seriously. 'I was looking forward to your company.'

She bit her lip. It had been stupid to go back on her word, especially as she wanted to attend the party. And now Jake was also unhappy—or at least, disappointed.

'I can't go now—not after telling Rohan I've changed my mind.'

'You'd like to go?' he inquired eagerly.

Dominie nodded her head.

'I would, yes.'

'Then I'll phone Rohan——'

'He'll think I'm stupid!'

'Didn't he say himself that it's a woman's prerogative to change her mind? Well, you've changed it again.'

The gardens of Windward Crest were softly illuminated by lights in the trees and the pool, like that of Jake's, was lit from underneath with coloured electric lamps that turned slowly, so that the blues and crimsons and various other colours mingled with the most delightful effect. Fringing the sides of the pool were exotic trees and shrubs like the lovely flamboyant, or Royal poinciana tree with its spectacular show of blooms covering the widespread limbs and, individually, resembling orchids; or the pink-blossomed frangipani with its delicious perfume. There were flowers with names like Flame of the Woods, Snow of the Mountains, Golden Candle and Shoot of Paradise. Colour and perfume and fairy-lights all combined to give the impression of a breathtakingly beautiful stage setting. It was too romantic by far, decided Dominie, who, clad in a pretty blue and white beach robe, very, very short, soon found herself beside her host, looking up into eyes that seemed, incredibly, to be laughing at her. He had sought her out almost at once, and here they were, at one end of the pool, away from the other guests. Her throat seemed to contract; she said hastily, and a trifle breathlessly,

'This is marvellous! I've never seen anything quite like it, not even on the pictures!'

74

'Nervous?' he queried, ignoring her comments. There was mockery in his voice. With a sort of stunning enlightenment Dominie knew that he was flirting with her. But what of Sylvia? Had he given up the chase ... having sighted another quarry?

'I don't know what you mean,' she faltered. 'Why should I be nervous?'

'Perhaps I should have said, unsure of yourself——'

'Nonsense! I'm never unsure of myself, Mr de Arden!'

He laughed, an attractive, low-pitched laugh which sent her pulses racing.

'Rohan,' he said briefly and, taking her arm, led her to a more secluded place, away from the pool, and the people swimming there. 'Say it,' he commanded imperiously. 'Well? Why the hesitation?'

She said, automatically wrapping her coat around her in a sort of protective action,

'You're a most puzzling man, Mr de Arden——'

'Only at first—not when you get to know me. Rohan, I said!'

'We're practically strangers.'

'You've known me almost as long as you've known Jake. You never had any difficulty with his name.'

'I met him on the ship. Everything's informal there. You all use Christian names.'

'We do here too.'

She glanced around; somehow, Rohan had managed to isolate them altogether from the rest. The pool was some distance away, and they were under a huge pouli tree, lavishly covered with pinkish-rose blossoms. Lighting was dim in this corner of the garden; although the moon was almost full it was partly obscured by soft white cloud.

75

'Don't you think,' she began nervously, 'that we should be getting back to the others?'

'We've only just left them. What's the hurry?'

'Mr de Arden——'

'You might find it easier,' he said, moving close, 'when I've kissed you—— No, my dear,' he laughed as she would have escaped, 'it's too late for you to run away.' And the next moment she was in his arms, enclosed in an inescapable embrace, and those sensuous lips claimed her in a long and passionate kiss.

'Oh ... you detestable creature!' she cried on being released. 'To—to do that—and without the least encouragement!' Indignant and angry though she was endeavouring to be, Dominie had to face the embarrassing fact that she failed miserably. Rohan's face was still close and even in the dim light she saw the amusement that lit those amber eyes.

'So you liked it. Good! Let's try again, shall we——?'

'No—certainly not! Let me go——!' She struggled on being caught to him again, but it was a futile effort and she gave it up. Triumphantly Rohan's mouth came down on hers, forcefully yet not in the least roughly, and after resisting his subtle persuasion and finesse for as long as she could Dominie forgot everything as she gave herself up to the sheer bliss of the moment. Vaguely she knew he would later despise her, and that she would despise herself, but she was helpless, held as she was, not only by his physical strength, but also by the personal charm and conquering force of the man.

'And now can you say my name?' he whispered, close to her ear.

'No—I—Rohan, please let me go!'

76

'Yes...' A moment's silence and then, 'It sounds exactly as I knew it would. Easy, wasn't it, Dominie?' Her name rolled off his tongue like a caress. Madness! He was insincere, a flirt, a profligate. He either ignored women or tempted them. She moved to release herself from his embrace, but his grip on her arms tightened. 'Why the haste?' His eyes laughed at her and there was a quiver to his mouth. 'You know, Dominie, it's not very flattering to my vanity when you want to rush off like this. Aren't you enjoying yourself?'

Colour flooded her cheeks, and her head lifted.

'Your vanity doesn't appear to be suffering overmuch,' she flashed. 'I find you pompous in the extreme!'

'I'm desolated! I imagined you were enjoying it as much as I.' He was mocking her, deriving a great deal of amusement from the situation. Dominie said, still acutely affected by his touch, and the nearness of him as once again he bent towards her,

'As you've had your enjoyment, perhaps we can go back to the pool. After all, it *was* supposed to be a swimming party ... if you remember?'

'Sarcasm too? Shall I give you that shaking I threatened you with?' No answer from Dominie. Rohan went on, looking at her in some amusement, 'Do you really want to go to the pool, I wonder? Wouldn't you rather stay here, alone with me?'

Dominie gave him a speaking glance, repeated that she found him pompous, and added for good measure,

'The pool will offer me much more pleasant amusement.'

'Liar! Why, if you didn't care for my kisses, did you reciprocate in so delightful a way?'

She was all confusion at this, not only because he spoke the truth but also because of those last few words. He sounded so sincere despite the mocking amusement edging his soft rich tones, and she knew a tingling of pleasure that he too had enjoyed those kisses. Dominie hadn't had much experience of men, always having been so busy, looking after her brother and the house, and working for a pay packet as well, and in responding to Rohan's lovemaking she had merely been following a natural instinct. He attracted her immensely; she had been happy to be in his arms, and it was gratifying to learn that Rohan also had been happy. She felt suddenly that she was not just 'another female' who was to be used for a moment's idle pleasure and then forgotten. Rohan spoke softly into her ear, repeating his question.

'Did—did I r-reciprocate?' she stammered, trying to twist out of his hold.

'You little wretch, Dominie. You prevaricating little wretch. You know darned well you did!' He paused a moment, waiting for her to speak, and continuing only after a long silence, 'What is it that's so different about you? What do you have that other women lack?' Holding her away from him, he gazed, half-frowning, into her eyes. Colour mounted her cheeks, fluctuating in the most captivating way, highlighting the perfect contours of her face. His words thrilled her even while some warning voice told her to beware. But she ignored it, held by Rohan in some exciting way that set her senses on fire and formed a barrier against all emotions except an intense yearning for him to kiss her again. Her lips parted and she tilted her head. With an intake of his breath Rohan stared, continuing to take in the enchanting picture for a long moment before, bending his head, he pressed his lips to hers. 'Dominie ... you bewitching creature ...'

She gave herself up to his kisses, living for the moment as ecstasy swept through her whole body.

'Rohan,' she whispered shyly when at last his lips left hers, 'people will be wondering where we are. And you—you shouldn't have left your guests for so long.' She was talking for the sake of talking, trying to take her mind off the tormenting question of whether or not Rohan was serious, or merely playing with her. She had nothing on which to assess his sincerity. He *sounded* sincere, it was true, but Dominie could not help doubting that a man like Rohan, who could choose any woman he wanted, would be seriously interested in her. Jake had asserted quite firmly that he would never stoop to using one woman in order to make another jealous, and after all Jake knew Rohan well. What had happened tonight was definitely not designed to make Sylvia jealous, so surely there was some meaning to it.

'You're right, my dear, we must go.' Rohan gave a small sigh and let her go. Five minutes later they were in the pool, mingling with the other swimmers, and later still they were with Jake, eating barbecued chicken and drinking rum punches under the moon.

'Where did you and Rohan disappear to for so long?' Jake wanted to know when at last he and Dominie were in his car, covering the short distance to Sunset Lodge. 'You can't say the attention he gave you tonight had anything to do with making Sylvia jealous.'

'He was showing me the gardens.'

'In the dark?'

Dominie blushed in the dimness of the car.

79

'We stopped and chatted for a while.'

'You're liking him better now, apparently?'

'Yes,' she answered quietly, 'I'm liking him much better now.'

CHAPTER FIVE

AN eager smile leapt to Dominie's face as Rohan came striding towards her after parking his car some short distance away. It was Saturday noon; Dominie had been shopping and Rohan had arranged to meet her at Bluebeard's Castle where they would have lunch together. Jake had taken the children on a visit to his sister who lived in Florida, and he would have taken Dominie too, but, aware of the way things were progressing between her and Rohan, he had obligingly told her she could have the week off work.

'All the shopping done?' Rohan reached her as she stood at the entrance to the building, which had once been a fortress but was now a luxury hotel. 'It would seem so, judging by the bulging bag you're carrying.' He took the gay embroidered shopping bag from her and said he had better put it in the car.

'I've spent up! Rohan, there are such wonderful things to buy!' She was deliriously happy; her eyes glowed and her cheeks were flushed. Her fair curls, although set attractively at the hairdressers only a couple of hours ago, were a trifle awry, the result of the caressing Caribbean trades, which blew almost all the time, bringing a welcome cooling influence to this tropical climate. 'Shall I walk back to the car with you?'

'Of course.' His low voice held an almost tender note and Dominie thrilled to it, as she did to the expression in his eyes. It seemed like a miracle that he should care for her, yet she was sure he did. True, he had never yet mentioned love, but then only ten days had elapsed since that night when, at the swimming party, he had kissed her. He had come over to Sunset Lodge almost every day since then, and twice he had taken her out to dine, the first time being to the Hotel 1829, where she had been pleasantly surprised to find century-old beams and colonial furniture. A charming bar had been made from the old kitchen; there was an attractive Spanish staircase and there were exotic flowers everywhere. Dominie had tasted her first lobster cooked West Indian style, from the charcoal grill. The second occasion on which he took her out was to the Carib Beach Hotel. From the silver sands of its beach they had stood looking out over the marvellous view of Lindbergh Bay, to Mosquito Point beyond. They had dined, and danced to the native orchestra till the early hours; they had strolled hand in hand through the tropical gardens, then driven home under a starlit sky, leaving the Caribbean as they crossed the island to the Atlantic side. Rohan had driven her to Sunset Lodge where, before seeing her safely inside, he had held her close, and they had remained on the terrace for a long while, enfolded in the warmth and peace of the soft tropical night.

'You're so lovely ... and so different,' he had murmured, and Dominie found it almost impossible to believe that he had once called her a little mouse. She sometimes fell to thinking of Sylvia, but the girl seemed unimportant now—just someone with whom Rohan would have amused himself had not Dominie

81

come on the scene.

With the shopping bag put in the car Rohan took her arm and they walked back to the Castle where they ate a delicious buffet lunch and listened to the gay and sparkling calypso singers.

'I must bring you here in the evening,' Rohan promised, 'and you can dance in the Pirate's Parlour.'

Dominie laughed.

'A pirate really did live here, Jake tells me?'

'That's right. You're in buccaneering territory now. Bluebeard lived in the Tower, from where he could spot the gold-laden galleons which were sailing from the New World to Europe. He was a lusty, handsome man with a thick beard that shone blue against his weathered cheeks when he faced a bright light. It was said he could polish off a gallon of rum at one go, without any noticeable effect.'

'What happened to him? Was he hanged?'

'He just disappeared, after stabbing his wife with a cutlass.'

'What times they were—exciting times!'

'And dangerous. Everyone was after everyone else's gold.' Rohan looked up as a woman approached their table. 'I seem to know that face,' he murmured, almost to himself.

'May I sit down for a moment?' asked the woman, and without waiting for permission she took possession of a spare chair. 'You don't remember me, Mr de Arden?'

'I'm sorry ... Why, yes, I do remember you. You were at Jake's place once when I was there.'

She smiled, glanced at Dominie and paused a moment before speaking.

'I shouldn't have intruded,' she apologized, but

made no effort to rise. 'Yes, I met you at the Harrises' about seven years ago.' Another pause. 'How are they?' she inquired slowly.

After introducing Dominie to Mrs Edgley Rohan told the woman that Mrs Harris had died a few months previously.

'Died? But she was so young—thirty-four, I think.'

'About that age, yes. Are you on holiday, Mrs Edgley?'

'Yes; I flew in a week ago. I'm here for another fortnight.' She paused again and Dominie looked at her, noting the rather attractive features and very dark eyes and hair. She was about forty-five years of age, Dominie estimated, although she had the figure of a young girl. 'How is Jake?—I mean, is he dreadfully upset by his wife's death?'

Rohan made no immediate reply, and when he did his accents seemed a little cold.

'I wouldn't know, Mrs Edgley.'

Dominie glanced swiftly at him, wondering why he hadn't mentioned the fact that Jake and his wife had been separated for five and a half years before her death. She felt it was not dislike of the woman that had caused his reticence, and realized almost immediately that Rohan was not the man to discuss his friend's private life with a comparative stranger.

'He's still at Sunset Lodge?'

'He's still there, but he's away from home at present.'

'Oh...' Mrs Edgley's disappointment was clearly portrayed in her expression. 'When will he be back?'

'In about three or four days' time.'

The woman's face cleared.

'I think I shall call on him,' she said, and rose from

83

the chair. 'I hope you didn't mind my speaking to you, Mr de Arden?'

'Not at all,' he returned graciously. 'I hope you'll enjoy your holiday.'

'Thank you,' she murmured, and walked away, over to a table in the corner, where she was lunching alone.

Dominie bit her lip.

'We could have asked her to join us,' she said.

'I suppose we could.' Rohan followed the direction of Dominie's gaze. 'It's too late; we've almost finished and, by the look of things, so has she. The waiter's just brought her the cheese board.'

'She seemed rather nice,' commented Dominie, and a twinkle entered her companion's eyes.

'A woman's curiosity, eh? Why don't you ask me outright who she is?'

Colour tinted Dominie's cheeks and she gave a small, deprecating laugh.

'All right, then. Who is she?'

'I believe she was once keen on Jake. Doreen, Jake's wife, didn't like the idea of her visiting them. I seem to recall that she had a fit of the sulks after Mrs Edgley had left.'

'Mrs Edgley's husband—is he not living with her?'

'He died about three years after their marriage.'

Dominie frowned, and glanced at the woman again.

'That was hard luck.'

'I don't think it was a love match.' Rohan shrugged carelessly. 'Jake said something, at the time, about the man being old enough to be her father, and that she had married him for security.'

'I feel sorry for her, somehow,' said Dominie after a pause. 'She looks lonely.'

Rohan smiled and said,

'What a silly girl you are—troubling your lovely head about a woman you don't even know.'

'If she was in love with Jake, and then lost him to someone else...' Dominie's eyes shadowed as once again she glanced at the woman. 'It—it must be crucifying.' She stopped suddenly. The last sentence had come without her thinking beforehand, and a warm flush of embarrassment began to rise in her cheeks as Rohan's eyes took on a faintly amused expression. But his voice was grave as he said,

'I notice you didn't speak in the past tense. Were you thinking of yourself, Dominie?'

Her flush deepened. This was plain speaking indeed. How must she answer him?

At length she found herself saying, her eyes frank and wide as they looked into his across the table.

'I admit I was thinking aloud, Rohan. If—if I were to fall in love, and then lose the man to another woman, I think I should die...' She allowed her voice to fade into silence, for her innermost hopes and desires had now been revealed, put into words that could not possibly be taken to mean anything but the truth ... that she was in love with Rohan. She felt hot inside, would have given anything to be able to withdraw those words, to go back in time just a few short moments.

Rohan was silent, watching her fluctuating colour, noting the spasmodic movement of her fingers as they fumbled with the pastry fork lying close to her plate. She lowered her eyes, avoiding his gaze, wondering what his thoughts were, and if he were regretting her confession because he himself could not reciprocate. The silence lasted so long that she raised her eyes at last, and he saw the tears glistening on her lashes. His hand went across the table and covered hers, gripping her fingers so that they were stilled.

'I love you, Dominie,' he said simply, and as she stared at him in wonderment, the tears being allowed to fall, then swept surreptitiously away, he added with a tender smile not untinged with amusement, 'I had different ideas about telling you, my darling ... a romantic setting with all the exotic island flavour of flowers and a moon and stars, but you're forced it from me, for I can't bear to see you unhappy. We know very little about one another,' he continued after she had offered him a tremulous little smile in place of words that just would not come, 'but we'll catch up. This afternoon we'll go home to Windward Crest and sit in the garden exchanging confidences. I want to know everything about you—everything, my dearest love.'

Her eyes, still moist, glowed with happiness. Moving her fingers as his grip slackened, she allowed them to curl round his, oblivious of any interested spectator who might be watching.

'I d-don't know what to say,' she murmured huskily, pulling her hand away at last.

'Just say you love me,' he returned with tender accents, and Dominie willingly obliged, though with shy hesitancy at first, and in tones almost inaudible which brought from Rohan the rather imperative request for a repetition. She laughed then and said obediently,

'I love you, Rohan.'

'Prettily spoken,' he teased, and then, glancing at her plate, 'Eat, my child. You might at this moment have other ideas, but I assure you it's impossible to live on love alone.'

She laughed again and looked down at her plate. Eat. Impossible when she was still so acutely affected by the miracle that had just occurred. Apologetically she glanced at him, shaking her head.

'I'm not hungry any more,' she began when a lift of his finger cut her short.

'Finish your sweet,' he ordered, but gently, and added that she might as well begin right away getting used to obeying her husband.

'Husband——' The word slipped out and she went red. 'It s-sounds w-wonderful,' she added shakily, avoiding his laughing regard.

'I wonder what Jake will think,' Dominie was saying an hour later as they were driving to Windward Crest, Rohan at the wheel of his car.

'He'll probably be mad at the idea of losing you so soon,' was the unconcerned reply as he turned on to the Hull Bay Road and the whole vista of islets and sea were spread out before them. 'He'll be having to look round for another nanny for the children.'

'He once said that you should be married, and have children of your own, since you like them so much.' Dominie spoke with a tinge of shyness, but only a tinge. She felt she and Rohan had known each other for a long time and now that she was no longer tormented by the uncertainty of his feelings for her, she was at complete ease with him, which was how it should be.

'So you've been talking about me behind my back, have you?'

'Susie mentioned you, on the ship, and as she called you uncle I naturally thought that Jake had a brother. He explained that you were just a friend.'

Rohan said nothing; they were almost at his home and Dominie sat back, taking in the lovely views. Bougainvillaea hedges grew beneath the flowering trees, which covered the hillsides, while in the other direction shone the dark blue Atlantic Ocean, with the islands of St. John and the British Virgins in the background. Along the mountain road itself were distanced out the magnificent house of the wealthy Americans who had settled on the island of St Thomas, escaping from the rat race and the keeping up with the Joneses and such things as bumper-to-bumper driving. Here was peace and slow tempo, with the world's most ideal climate thrown in for good measure. Tropical gardens surrounded almost every villa, and swimming-pools could be glimpsed now and then, shining through the trees. Every entrance was a picture, with ornamental gates and stonework and lamps on pillars. An incongruous note was struck in each instance by the rather ramshackle letter-box perched on a post on the verge outside the gate. No one had bothered to make these look pretty; they were made out of what appeared to be rough wooden boxes, with a piece of tin perched on top as protection against the rain.

'Here we are, my love ... home.' Rohan turned to throw her a slanting glance and her heart seemed to ache with happiness, for no man had ever looked with more tenderness at his beloved.

The car slid to a halt outside the house and a native servant came at once and drove it off, to the garage which was well away, out of sight of the house. Dominie looked up at Rohan and shook her head faintly. 'I can't believe it's true,' she said, but to herself.

She had talked about herself for over half an hour, answering the questions Rohan several times put to her, and now she had fallen silent, her face sad as she thought of Jerry and wished so much that he too could be appreciating the beauty of this island. Rohan leant forward in his garden chair and took her hand.

'I know just how you feel at the loss,' he said, and she saw his mouth tighten into an ugly line, revealing to her that the man she was to marry possessed an altogether different side to his nature than the most attractive one she had seen. 'I lost my sister in a road accident——' He stopped, then added, 'Perhaps Jake mentioned this to you?'

She nodded.

'Yes, he did. She was killed about the same time as Jerry, I believe?'

'The same day, it would seem. But it was in the evening when my accident occurred and therefore quite dark. The woman driver who caused the accident was drunk, and although she stopped momentarily, she then drove off and we never found out who she was.'

'Drunk...' Dominie shook her head, her big blue eyes sad still, but compassionate too, for she knew a deep sympathy for him. 'It's criminal the way people drink and drive. I expect she'd been to some party or other.' She paused, reflecting on the questions Rohan had asked about Jerry, and wondering if she should ask Rohan to talk about his sister. She said at length, hesitantly, 'Do you want to tell me about Alicia?'

Bitterness fell like a mask on his features. He seemed all at once to be frozen inside.

'She was a lovely girl,' he said at last, broodingly and quietly, as if totally absorbed in a mood of reflection. 'And she had the most charming personality—I'm not just saying this, Dominie. She really was exceptional in every way. One can never understand why a young person like that should fall victim to a wretch who would get herself into a drunken state and then take a car on to the road.' The ugly twist marred his features again and involuntarily Dominie shivered. She recalled Jake's saying that Rohan would have killed the woman, could he have found her, and, looking at him now, with his handsome face twisted almost evilly, and one hand, resting on the arm of his chair, opening and closing with the sort of movement that conjured up pictures of strangulation, Dominie sent up a fervent prayer that fate would never bring about a meeting between the two.

Rohan was speaking again, recounting to Dominie what had happened on that fateful evening—how the car had come from a side road into the main road without even slowing down, how Rohan had hit the lamp standard in his endeavour to avoid a collision.

'Alicia hit the side of the door with her head and died instantly. She knew nothing, but that's little consolation to me. A young life was lost through the criminal action of that woman, and she got away with it— she's free to do the same again, to kill someone else.' The bitterness in his voice was terrible to hear, and Dominie could not speak while he was so encompassed in the retrospection from which that bitterness was born. She felt miserable and it showed in the shadows which filled her eyes. Time passed and Rohan continued to brood, but suddenly he seemed to become aware of her presence and jerked himself from his unhappy reverie.

'Darling——' He took her hand again, and lifted it to his lips. 'I'm sorry. It isn't often that I dwell on the tragedy these days——' He stopped again and spread his hand. 'It's past, and best forgotten—yet it's hard sometimes to forget, the circumstances being what they were.'

She nodded and after a thoughtful moment admitted that it was not quite so bad for her. The accident which killed Jerry had been unavoidable on the lorry driver's part, since he skidded on a very icy road and although he had made a desperate effort to regain control of his vehicle he had found it impossible.

'Unlike you, darling,' she added, putting his hand to her cheek in a little tender gesture, 'I don't have to live with the knowledge that the accident was caused by a criminal act on the part of the other driver.'

Rohan changed the subject, beginning to talk about his mother, and Dominie listened, not mentioning that Jake had already told her a little about the affair.

'The girl was half Mother's age,' Rohan added, a harsh note creeping into his voice. 'What she and a man of fifty could have in common I don't know. She was a strumpet if ever there was one!'

'I expect these occurrences turned you against women.' Dominie wondered it he would mention Nina, the girl whom everyone expected him to marry.

'They did.' Rohan's brow cleared of the slight frown that had settled on it; he produced his very attractive smile, and his amber eyes twinkled. 'Then you came along and swept away all my intentions of remaining a bachelor.'

Her eyes met his. She couldn't help saying,

'Sylvia ... you seemed to like her very much.'

His smile faded. He seemed lost for a moment in thought. Dominie felt that if he spoke what was in his mind she would hear that he considered Sylvia to be merely a spoiled child who fully intended marrying for money. Instead, she heard him say, casually and with the sort of firm inflection that conveyed to Dominie that it was not his intention to discuss Sylvia at any length,

'I got to know her through her father, with whom I've recently done a good deal of business. One day she'll make a pretty addition to some rich man's home, but for myself I want more than what satisfies the eye —for a wife, that is.'

Dominie flushed adorably and lowered her lashes. She was recalling the conversation she had overhead and now knew for sure that Rohan's interest in the girl had gone no deeper than that which was physical. An affair he would have enjoyed; marriage had never for one moment entered his mind. She looked at him, noting the clearly-defined features, arrogant even when they were softened by his smile, as they were at this moment. She took in the straight, aristocratic shoulders, the leanness of his body which denoted a hidden strength. She caught her breath, all her mind and body being affected by his unfailing charm. How had she, a little nobody whose life's routine had been the office from nine till five and then household chores, come to attract a man like this? For one rather frightening moment she felt it could not be true, that she would awake suddenly from a beautiful dream, to find herself back in the old mundane surroundings where the odd visit to a friend was the only diversion.

Rohan said, rather sharply,

'What are you thinking, Dominie? You look far from happy.'

Her head jerked. She hesitated momentarily, then was honest with him.

'I felt I might awake from this lovely dream and— and find you gone.'

His tender, reassuring voice answered her.

'You and I won't ever lose each other very easily. I've been a long time meeting up with the girl I want for my wife, but now that I have, it's for always.' And then she was in his arms, surrendering her lips gladly to his, while all around them the soft tropical breeze wafted delicious perfumes over the air. Flower jewels like the Bird of Paradise with its brilliant orange sepals flickering like flames, or the Snow Pillow—that breathtaking white poinsettia—or the passion flowers with their bursts of blue and white and purple filaments, made provocative pictures whose settings were the palms and the breadfruit trees which themselves were framed against a sapphire sky lightly flecked with the fleecy clouds that shone like silver, touched as they were by the sun's clear rays. Far down below the calm blue waters of the Atlantic invaded the beautiful sweeping curve of Magens Bay which, forming an almost symmetrical 'U', terminated in Tropaco Point at one end and Picara Point at the other. Islands glistened in the sun—Hans Lollik and Jost Van Dyck, St John and the British Virgins.

Released at last from her lover's embrace, Dominie scanned the dazzling vista for a long moment before bringing her eyes to the more immediate scene of a lawn cut by parterres, of high clipped hibiscus hedges, and luxuriant flowering trees sweeping away to the rise which was in effect a semi-wild garden of 'planned design'. She closed her eyes suddenly and pressed close to Rohan.

His words had had meaning; his embrace was reassuringly hard and possessive ... and yet a shiver passed through her ... a shiver of apprehension and foreboding.

CHAPTER SIX

It had been Dominie's intention to inform Jake of her engagement immediately on his return, and at the same time ask him to find someone to replace her. But the moment he arrived she took one look at his drawn pinched face and said,

'Are you ill, Jake? You look as if you should be in bed.' Even the children were quiet, both looking up at their father through wide anxious eyes. 'What's wrong? You've lost a lot of weight.'

He nodded listlessly.

'I caught some sort of a bug over there and my sister called the doctor. He wanted me to enter hospital, but I decided to try and get home. My sister also got the bug, but was not so ill as I. However, it prevented her making too much fuss when I decided to come away. I expect it's something we ate—although the doctor was baffled by our condition.' He gave a shuddering sigh and it was obvious to Dominie that he felt cold. 'I'm going to bed, dear, and I expect I shall be right again in a day or two.'

'I must ring your doctor,' she returned in firm decisive tones. 'Don't worry about a thing, Jake. Just get into bed and relax.'

'I haven't asked how you've gone on while I've been away,' he murmured apologetically. 'Rohan took you out a great deal, I suppose?'

'Yes, Jake, he did.' She had no intention of mentioning anything else at this time, as Jake must be spared any unnecessary anxiety while he was so ill. 'Now,' she added briskly, 'off you go. I'll come up when you're in bed and see if there's anything you want. Meanwhile,

I'll ring the doctor.'

She rang Rohan as well, and he appeared on the scene within ten minutes, having come by car.

'Is it serious?' he asked, scanning her face. 'You sounded greatly perturbed just now.'

'I feel it, Rohan,' she frowned. 'He looks awful.'

'I'll go up——' He turned on his way to the door. 'The doctor's coming?'

'He was out, but I was assured he would come to Jake immediately on his return.'

Rohan's mouth tightened, then relaxed.

'There's nothing else we can do. I don't expect it will be too long before he arrives.'

'Uncle Rohan,' interrupted Susie in a voice edged with tears, 'is my daddy very ill?'

Rohan patted her fair head, then, with her small face in his hand, he pressed her to him for a second.

'He'll be all right, Susie, so there's no need for tears. All you have to do is be good, and on no account must you worry your father, understand?'

She nodded vigorously.

'We won't go up to his bedroom unless Auntie Dominie tells us we can, will we, Geoffrey?'

Geoffrey's lips were tight.

'I want to have my daddy downstairs. I don't like him being in bed——'

'You heard me,' in rather stern tones from Rohan. 'You go up only when you're told you can. Is that clear?'

Reluctantly the boy nodded. Soothingly Dominie told him to go out in the garden and play with Susie.

'We'll all go up and sit with Daddy later—if the doctor says we can,' she promiseed, and both children smiled then, seeming to be reassured by her gentle tones, and her smile. But she herself was troubled; Jake had looked very ill indeed when, for a few moments between her telephoning and the arrival of Rohan, she had stood beside his bed. His face seemed even more drawn and thin, and he scarcely noticed that she was there, his eyes being closed, and his forehead damp with perspiration.

'I don't like the look of him at all,' Rohan was saying a few minutes later. 'He seemed to get worse even while I stood there. If only we could get hold of that doctor!' He stopped and then, with sudden decision, 'We'll find out where he is!'

After telephoning the doctor's residence Rohan then made another call, catching Dr Hooper before he left the house of the patient he was visiting.

'You've got him?' Dominie spoke even before Rohan had replaced the receiver.

'Yes; he'll come here next.' Rohan's voice was grim; his eyes strayed to the two children playing on the lawn. It wasn't difficult to read his thoughts and Dominie swallowed hard, trying to remove the blockage that had risen in her throat.

Dr Hooper arrived twenty minutes later and Rohan took him up to Jake's room, which was darkened, as Dominie had drawn the curtains, shutting out the fierce tropical sun. It seemed an eternity before the two men came back into the sitting-room where Dominie waited, her heart beating over-rate and her mind dwelling all the time on what might happen.

'Frankly,' the doctor was saying as they came through the arched doorway separating the room from the entrance hall, 'I don't know what it is, Mr de Arden. As I've just said, I'm arranging for him to enter hospital.'

'Is it something very serious, Doctor?' Dominie spoke without thinking, so great was her anxiety, and she was not surprised when Dr Hooper gave a small sigh of impatience.

'I don't know,' he answered abruptly, and Rohan intervened, in his quiet, accented voice,

'We're troubled, as you must understand, and naturally we're wanting to know just what's wrong with Mr Harris.'

'I do understand,' shortly and followed by another sigh of impatience. 'I wish I knew myself what's wrong with him.' He appeared vexed at his inability to produce a diagnosis and Rohan understandingly told him that the doctor in Florida had also been baffled by Jake's illness.

He went with the doctor to the door and when he rejoined Dominie his face was as troubled as hers.

'You didn't mention anything about your leaving?' he asked, nodding approvingly as Dominie shook her head.

'We'll have to keep our engagement a secret,' she said, and although Rohan frowned slightly at this he had to agree.

'If we let it be known generally it's bound to come back to him, as he's sure to be having numerous visitors while he's in hospital.' Crossing over to her, Rohan took her hands in his. 'I hadn't any intention of waiting, my love,' he said tenderly, 'but it seems I must.' Bending his head, he kissed her on the lips. 'I'd marry you tomorrow were it at all possible,' he told her, but Dominie found herself quite unable to be thrilled by these words. Not only was she prevented from doing so by her anxiety over Jake, but also by a recurrence of that foreboding she had experienced on a previous occasion and which, for some inexplicable reason, was vastly increased by this necessary secrecy over the engagement. It was as if a great shadow were pressing down on her, slowly but surely enveloping her in darkness.

'The children are going to be upset,' she said, forced to change the subject, in the hope that she could transmute her fears merely to disappointment, which would be a much more natural, and understandable, emotion. 'I don't quite know how to tell them that their father is to go into hospital.'

'I'll tell them,' offered Rohan without hesitation and, going over to the window, he tapped on it and beckoned to them. They came running in at once; Rohan took them to the couch and they sat down, one on either side of him. Dominie waited long enough to see him slip an arm around each, and then she quietly left the room.

Two hours after Jake's removal to hospital, which was less than a mile and a half from Sunset Lodge, Dominie glanced up to see Mrs Edgley coming up the path which, running at right angles to the main drive, led to the part of the garden in which Dominie was sitting, reading to the children, both of whom were at her feet, seated on a rug which Dominie had spread upon the grass.

'I heard your voice,' the woman said, 'so I came to you first. Is Jake in? I'd like to see him—but if he's busy, or anything...?' Mrs Edgley spread her hands in a little nervous gesture. 'I wouldn't want to disturb him if he's working. I seem to recall that his wife said he was always in his study.'

Looking up at the woman from her brightly-covered

garden chair, Dominie felt puzzled by her manner. On the surface Mrs Edgley appeared to possess her fair share of confidence, yet she was obviously nervous and uncomfortable and Dominie sensed that this resulted from the fear that Jake might not be pleased to see her. She, on the other hand, seemed more than anxious to see him, and the additional impression that came to Dominie was that the woman had actually forced herself to make this visit.

'I'm sorry, Mrs Edgley, but Jake was taken to hospital about two hours ago. He returned from his trip to Florida this morning and went straight to bed, as he'd been ill while he was away. The doctor was sent for and ordered him to enter hospital. They don't know what's wrong with him,' she added, anticipating Mrs Edgley's question before she could voice it.

'In hospital...?' The woman's face had paled slightly. 'It's serious?'

'We don't know, Mrs Edgley. The doctor could tell us nothing. I have to ring the hospital this evening.' A strange feeling of pity rose within Dominie; she recalled that this had occurred on her first meeting with the woman. Did she still care for Jake? And was she cherishing the hope that, now he was widowed, she might stand a chance? It would seem so, decided Dominie, watching the woman's mouth as it trembled slightly, despite her obvious effort to prevent it.

'So you don't know how long he'll be in there?' And when Dominie shook her head, 'It's fate,' the woman murmured to herself. 'We're not to meet.' She looked up and her eyes had taken on an unnatural brightness. 'I shouldn't have come,' she quivered. 'I—I hope Jake will be all right—for the children's sake. I'm sorry to have troubled you, Miss Worthing.' Turning away, she said huskily, over her shoulder, 'Good afternoon. Please don't mention my visit to Jake.'

'Mrs Edgley!' Impulsively Dominie let out the exclamation and the woman twisted round. Her pretty face was puckered; she looked more like a child than a woman approaching middle age. 'Can I offer you some lunch——? No, please don't refuse. We usually have ours at one o'clock, and it's almost that time now.'

'But the—the trouble,' she began, when Dominie interrupted her.

'It's no trouble at all,' said Dominie, rising from her chair. 'Do stay, Mrs Edgley. I'll go and have another place laid for you.'

'You're very kind.' The low sweet voice was not quite steady, but the hazel eyes had taken on a happier look. 'The children,' she murmured, glancing at their upturned faces, 'you were reading to them.'

'They don't mind if I stop now.' Dominie gave them a smile and they instantly responded. 'Do you, my pets?'

'No,' from Susie, but hesitantly, and then, 'Can this lady read a bit more to us, while you go and tell Molly that she's staying for lunch?'

'Well . . .?' Dominie looked questioningly at their visitor, who eagerly accepted the invitation Susie had offered.

'May I have your chair?' she added, preparing to sit down.

'Of course.' Dominie moved away, an unaccountable lightness having entered into her, and she dwelt on this through lunch, which was taken in the elegantly-furnished dining-room whose main windows faced the mountain scene, and whose side window gave on to a vista of colourful terraced gardens sweeping down to the palm-fringed swimming-pool.

'Jake has a magnificent place here.' Mrs Edgley's voice brought Dominie from her private thoughts. She had been trying to find a reason for this strange lightness of spirit, but with the intrusion she gave up the attempt, politely offering Mrs Edgley her whole attention. The children, who had been quietly talking to one another, both looked up as their visitor spoke, and it was Susie who responded to what she had said.

'Do you like it? We love it here—but we haven't always lived with Daddy, you know. We lived with Mummy most of the time, in England, and we stayed with Daddy only for July and August every year since I can remember.'

'With Mummy?' A swift glance in Dominie's direction, but although Dominie braced herself for the question it was held back, for which Dominie was thankful, having no desire to discuss her employer with Mrs Edgley who was, after all, an almost complete stranger to her. But Susie, with typical childish frankness and lack of tact, very soon answered the unspoken question and Mrs Edgley, learning of the separation, did then venture to put a question or two to her hostess.

'Were they separated for long, Miss Worthing?'

'About five and a half years.' A pause, and then, 'I'm not really in Jake's confidence. I met him only around Christmas time; we were travelling on the same ship——'

'Daddy was bringing us here, to live with him,' interrupted Geoffrey, his small mouth full of food. 'It was a cruise, but Auntie Dominie missed it because she came to stay with us for a little while.'

'She missed the ship,' explained Susie after first telling her brother that he must not speak with his mouth full. 'Our car went wrong and Daddy asked Uncle Rohan to take her to the ship, but when they got there it was sailing away!'

'We were glad, weren't we, Sue?'

'Yes, because Auntie Dominie couldn't go home.'

'I did eventually go home,' she reminded them, having decided it was too late to quieten them, as already they had said sufficient to give Mrs Edgley a fair picture of Jake's marriage.

'But you soon came back, so that you could mind us.'

'That's how it happened?' smiled Mrs Edgley, and Dominie nodded.

'I hadn't any real ties in England, and as I liked the children, and they seemed to like me, I accepted Jake's offer.' She was thinking of Rohan, and the way she had been drawn to him after first disliking him excessively, mainly because of the conversation she had overheard. It was strange, she mused, that Rohan's first impression of her should have caused him to dub her a little mouse, and even now she flushed uncomfortably at the recollection. Of course, at the time he had been endeavouring to persuade the girl into a situation which suited his desires, and with this aim in view he was also trying to convince her that no other woman could have any attraction for him. Little he knew, at that time, how close he was to falling in love with the girl of whom Sylvia spoke, and whom he had so casually dismissed as unimportant.

Sylvia ... Several times Dominie had wondered how she would take the engagement. She had wanted to marry Rohan, but she was not in love with him, Dominie was absolutely sure of that.

'It's lucky for Jake that you're here at this time,' Mrs

Edgley was remarking as she leant back in her chair, dabbing her mouth with her napkin. Dominie merely nodded and after a small pause Mrs Edgley continued on a little wistful note, 'You must enjoy looking after two such delightful children. It was always a deep regret of mine that I never had any.'

'Children are nice to have around,' agreed Dominie, going on to ask if Mrs Edgley had had enough to eat. 'You've not taken very much,' she ended, with a glance at the portion of delicious sherry trifle left on Mrs Edgley's plate.

'I have to watch my figure. I'm very stern with myself, for I've no intention of putting on weight and in consequence growing old before my time.'

On leaving the table the two children ran off into the garden, and Dominie ordered coffee for Mrs Edgley and herself to be served on the patio. 'They'd be at school in the normal way, I expect?' Mrs Edgley settled into the comfortable chair which Dominie pulled forward for her. 'They're at home today because of the visit to Florida?'

'That's right. It was after nine when they arrived home, having caught the early morning plane from Miami.' Bringing up a small table, Dominie placed it close to her visitor, and then sat down. 'They'll be at school tomorrow.'

The two chatted for a while, with Mrs Edgley becoming more confiding so that Dominie learned a good deal about her and, reading between the lines, fitted in a good deal more. Erica Greenwood, as she was then, had been thirty when she met and fell in love with Jake Harris who, at thirty-four, had recently met the lovely seventeen-year-old Doreen and begun going about with her.

'I suppose I would be termed the bitch,' Mrs Edgley said reminiscently. 'I wanted him so badly that I wished I could part them—yes, I freely admit it because, you see, I knew instinctively that they weren't suited. I felt that I could make him far happier than she ever could. But what chance has a woman of thirty with a lovely girl of seventeen? She won, and I faded out; I eventually got married—for companionship more than anything else, and for security. My husband and I never quarrelled; on the other hand, we were never really close. I was sorry when he died, but I was not grief-stricken.' Erica Edgley paused in thought and Dominie watched her changing expression as she lived through those not-too-happy years with the husband whom she had never loved. Dominie admired her honesty, refusing to regard her as the 'bitch' which she termed herself, for it was Dominie's own view that Erica would indeed have made Jake happy. She was sincere and frank; she was dainty and pretty, and she possessed a very charming way that even the children had noticed, for on Dominie's going to them as they washed their hands before going in to eat their lunch, both children had said she was 'nice'.

'She talks in a nice way, and her face is nice,' stated Susie, and her brother complemented with,

'She has a nice smile and her eyes are nice when they look at you.'

'It's some years since your husband died, I believe?'

'It's nine years.' Erica picked up her coffee cup and took a drink, her eyes wandering to where the children were playing with a huge, brightly-coloured beach ball on the lawn. 'I began to travel, and when a cruise ship I was on berthed here I couldn't resist the temptation to call and see how Jake and his wife were getting on.'

'You hadn't quarrelled with them, then?'

'No; we'd parted quite good friends. I once had a suspicion that Jake knew I cared for him, but he never knew that I would have come between them had I ever had the chance.'

'Were you living on St. Thomas at the time?'

'We all lived in New York. I was secretary to Jake's partner. Jake has since bought this man out. Now of course, the business has expanded, and become a large company. Jake bought this place about two years after he was married.' Erica replaced her cup and leant back in her chair, looking at Dominie. 'They seemed quite happy at the time I visited them,' she went on musingly. 'Susie was a delightful little thing—about fifteen months old. I adored her...' The words trailed away in a deep and yearning sigh and Dominie bit her lip till it hurt. 'Geoffrey wasn't born, of course. They were married several years before Susie was born,' she added, then lapsed into silence, her eyes straying once more to the children playing on the lawn.

Dominie said, not knowing from where the essence of her words had sprung,

'I wish it had been you he had chosen——' and just as suddenly as they were spoken, so the words were clipped off and Dominie was staring at her companion, the colour slowly rising in her cheeks. 'I'm sorry ... I didn't mean to hurt you.'

The woman smiled and shook her head.

'Don't apologize. It was kind of you to say that.'

'But not thoughtful. I know I've hurt you.'

'I'm beyond being hurt, Dominie—— I can call you Dominie, can't I?'

'I'd like you to,' she replied simply and, when Erica remained silent, 'Would you care to stay until I've phoned the hospital? You would know, then, if he can have visitors.'

The profound hush that fell was almost poignant in its intensity. It was broken by a long-drawn-out sigh before Erica murmured, her expressive hazel eyes misted by tears,

'Dominie ... it's such a long time since anyone was kind to me.' A lump rose in her throat and she fell silent, swallowing. 'Thank you,' she ended huskily, and reached in her pocket for a handkerchief.

'We eat at seven—because of the children,' Dominie informed her prosaically, yet blinking away the tears from her own eyes. 'If you like I'll show you a bedroom, with its bath, so that you can rest if you wish, and tidy up later.'

Erica merely inclined her head, and followed Dominie into the house. The room to which Dominie took her was decorated in two shades of lilac; the furniture was white. Embroidered net curtains billowed into the room as the Atlantic breeze filtered through the partly-open window. The view was to the gardens and the sea, the only sound that of the children's laughter drifting up from below.

Erica's eyes were still bright. Understandingly Dominie said,

'Perhaps you'd like that rest right now,' and, turning on her heel, she went out, and along to her own room where she stood, in the middle of the floor, wondering how she could be feeling lighthearted and sad at the same time. 'I'm sure—quite sure—that they'll get together,' she whispered, at last realizing why she was feeling this lightness of spirit. Subconsciously she had

now, take that frown off your face and give your lord and master a smile!'

The ache in her heart was healed by those words, and although she still retained an ache which had nothing to do with her own love, she managed to smile as ordered. But she did at the same time lift her chin and proceed to remind him that he was not yet her lord and master.

'And even when we're married,' she went on to tell him, 'I shall not be a meek little come-hither wife. I intend to have a will of my own!'

'Rebellion already!' His straight dark brows drew together in a frown. 'Shall I beat you into submission —or make love to you?'

Startled, she gave a rather shaky little laugh.

'I was only teasing,' she said.

'Scared now, are you? Yes, I think I shall make love to you, so that you'll know, for future reference, who's the master.'

After a nervous little cough Dominie said,

'Mrs Edgley—Erica—I was telling you about her. I do think that Jake might grow to care for her, no matter what you say to the contrary. She's awfully sweet, Rohan...' Her voice trailed off as Rohan burst out laughing. He stood up and drew her close against his hard and muscled body: she saw his head come down, felt the first touch of his lips that was no more than the caress of a breeze in summer ... and then she was possessed, her lips and her body; her very soul seemed to be stolen from her by his ardour and his strength.

'Rohan,' she gasped, trying to twist her body away after succeeding to free her lips. 'Please!'

At last he held her at a distance, his hands gentle on her arms, his eyes dark with suppressed passion and yet surprisingly retaining a hint of amusement in their depths.

'So ... I can scare you, it seems. Don't worry, my dear sweet love, I'll never harm you.' Tenderly he kissed her, then let his mouth caress her face and the lovely curve of her throat. 'Did I really frighten you, my darling?'

'J-just a little,' she owned, pressing her face into the gleaming whiteness of the cotton shirt he wore. 'Or perhaps,' she amended in a muffled voice, 'it was myself I was afraid of.'

'You ... darling!' And she was swept into the whirlpool of his ardour again, her soft breasts crushed against the iron-hardness of his chest, her mouth bruised under the mastery of his. She had asked for it, of course, and she made no effort at resistance this time, but gave herself up to the sheer undiluted rapture of the moment. But when his hand came from her back and would have cupped her breast she caught it swiftly and put it to her cheek. Softly he laughed, and drew away from her a little, so that he could look down into her eyes, eyes drowsy and darkly shadowed by the longing that was still intensely gripping her. 'My cautious little love ... I adore you!'

She gave a shy and quiet laugh, responding to his own.

'I love you dearly,' she whispered huskily. 'How much I cannot say, but all I know is that, in so short a time, you've become my very life. Without you I should die——'

'You'll never be without me—never!'

Mistily she looked into his eyes, searching them, probing, endeavouring to read his thoughts.

'Whatever happened ... you would still love me?'

What words were these to ask a lover? His voice, his expression, his caress, his tender roughness that was ardour held in check … all these were proof of enduring love, and yet that question had emerged from some tortured corner of her mind, to be voiced through lips that quivered almost piteously.

'Darling, what's the matter?' His anxious voice, tender-edged and low, was accompanied by a protective tightening of his arms again as Dominie was brought up close to him. 'This is for ever; you must know that. It's no shallow, purely physical attraction that we've found, but something so deep and lasting that it will endure until the very end.' His voice was grave now and so were his eyes. 'I have no doubts, my dearest, so why should you?'

'I'm silly,' she admitted, pressing her face into his shoulder. 'It's just that I'm so happy that I'm frightened.' She paused, waiting, but Rohan made no comment and she continued, 'I suppose a man thinks differently from a woman. He doesn't harbour stupid fears and doubts; he doesn't see pictures that aren't really there.'

'Pictures? What sort of pictures?'

She shrugged deprecatingly.

'Pictures of—of disaster,' she said at last, and received a little shake, and a smack.

'Stop being silly! I mean it, Dominie!' There was no softness about him now. On the contrary, his face was stern and set, his thrusting jaw flexed, his eyes flickering with a warning light. 'Snap out of it—do you hear?'

'Yes. I'm sorry…' She hated his mood, and she was angry with herself for causing it. 'D-don't be like this, Rohan.'

He softened then, and for a long moment she knew the thrill of his kisses again.

'Better now?' he asked gently, and she nodded.

'I don't know what came over me.'

'Probably pent-up emotions,' he said with a bluntness that made her blush. 'I hope it won't be too long before we can be married—— Don't be so embarrassed, my pet. It's natural. For myself, I want you now —this minute!'

CHAPTER SEVEN

BOTH to Dominie's disappointment and Erica's, Jake was not allowed visitors. He was comfortable, was the non-committal report received when Dominie telephoned the hospital. No, said the abrupt voice at the other end of the line, his illness had not yet been diagnosed.

'I have the sure conviction that I'm not to meet Jake.' Erica's voice was listless and edged with resignation. 'I'd like to keep in touch until I leave the island,' she added, glancing from Dominie to Rohan who had strolled over again after dinner—just to kiss Dominie goodnight, he said. 'I would be happy to know that he's getting better.'

'Of course you must keep in touch,' Dominie agreed, wishing Rohan would be a little more friendly towards Erica. He had no time for women who ran after men, he had earlier told his fiancée. It was the male who should do the hunting, as nature had ordained. 'Come whenever you like. I wish I could invite you to stay here, but I'm afraid I couldn't take it upon myself to go that far.' A sideways glance at Rohan revealed a lifting of his brows in a gesture of astonishment that Dominie should even mention such a thing as that of having Erica stay at Sunset Lodge in Jake's absence.

'It's kind of you to think of that, Dominie, but as you say, I can't stay here without Jake's permission. I'll accept your offer to come and see you, though. I'm alone, as you know, and it'll be pleasant to have your company now and then.' She looked at Rohan; his handsome face was impassive, and with a sort of urgency Erica rose and picked up her handbag from the couch where she had been sitting. 'I'll say good-night——' A smile fluttered; Erica seemed nervous and unsure of herself as she took a backward step towards the door. 'I'll call round tomorrow afternoon, if I may?'

'Come for lunch,' invited Dominie impulsively. 'There's no need to be on your own. I shall love to have you, and so will the children.'

The smile took on a more definite curve.

'I will come for lunch,' she decided, and went with Dominie to the front door. 'I don't think Mr de Arden approves of me,' she said quietly, and then she asked, before Dominie could find anything to say to that, 'Is he your young man?'

Dominie became guarded, her thoughts immediately flitting to the possibility of a meeting between Erica and Jake—a meeting which she, Dominie, intended to bring about if she could.

'He's just a friend, Erica. He's known Jake for years, and consequently he and Jake are regular visitors to one another's homes. He's exceedingly anxious about Jake at the present time.'

No more was said, except a final goodnight, and

after waiting until Erica had disappeared from view Dominie returned to the sitting-room where Rohan was standing by the window, looking stern. Sensing a reprimand, Dominie forestalled it by asking about Jake's wife.

'Was she a good mother?' Dominie added when Rohan had described Doreen as very lovely, with auburn hair and grey-green eyes.

'I believe so. Jake never complained about her treatment of the children, and they appeared to be happy enough——' He broke off, the stern expression still lingering on his face. 'I expect you want me to say she wasn't a good wife to Jake, and that Mrs Edgley would have made a better one? Well, as I have never asked for Jake's confidence on so intimate and personal a matter I wouldn't know.'

Dominie swallowed. She knew a surge of dejection as the idea occurred to her that Rohan might be a little disappointed in her, considering her to be a meddlesome female who could not mind her own business.

'Are you angry with me?' she asked at length, unable to bear the hurt any longer.

'I'm surprised that you should interfere in something that isn't your concern. As I've said, I have no time for women who do the chasing, and if the truth were known it would probably transpire that Mrs Edgley has no one else but herself to blame that Jake wanted nothing to do with her.'

'You're very unkind, Rohan,' Dominie could not help saying as the sad face of Erica rose up before her. 'A woman can't help it if she falls in love with a man. And it must have been true love she felt for Jake, otherwise it would have died before now.'

'Jake,' responded Rohan with quiet deliberation, 'is a very wealthy man.'

'Erica isn't interested in his money!'

'That might be your opinion; it doesn't happen to be mine.'

'She has money of her own.'

'Which is nothing in comparison.'

Dominie's colour rose; she was angry and unhappy at the same time. There seemed to be so many facets to the personality of this man whom she was to marry, and she did wonder if there would be numerous occasions on which he would hurt her, as he was hurting her now, by the hardness of his features and the abruptness of his tone. Suddenly she wanted to be alone, to have Rohan leave before this discussion developed into a quarrel.

'I'm tired,' she said, trying to blink away the prick of tears behind her eyes. 'I think I'll go to bed ... if you don't mind.'

Rohan stared, and as she watched a tiny gasp left her lips at the sudden transformation in his face. Tender lines erased the hardness round his mouth; the amber eyes softened and the voice was yielding and gentle as he said,

'Darling, we're not going to quarrel over this woman. She'll be gone in just over a week and we shall probably never set eyes on her again.' Crossing the room, Rohan took Dominie in his arms. 'Don't cry, my love—you mustn't!' His tender lips found hers; his kiss was reassuring and she shook off her unhappiness, smiling apologetically when a moment later he was gently drying her eyes with his handkerchief. 'I love you for your anxiety over Mrs Edgley,' he said unexpectedly, but went on to add that in his opinion any matchmaking plans Dominie had were doomed to failure. 'Forget all about them, my sweet, and give all your attention to your lover.'

Rohan was probably right, Dominie was telling herself when, the following morning at half-past eleven, she stood on the verandah and watched Erica coming along the path. Slender and youthful, Erica walked with a graceful, attractive swing. She seemed happier, even from this distance, and as she drew nearer Dominie noticed the half-smile on her lips.

'It's so nice to have somewhere to come to!' she exclaimed on reaching Dominie. 'It all seems so aimless, travelling about and sightseeing all the time——' She gave a shrug. 'And yet, when you're on your own, what else is there to do?'

Inwardly, Dominie gave a deep sigh. She wished she could make a friend of Erica, could help her to feel less lonely. But as Rohan had said, Erica would be gone quite soon and it was unlikely that their paths would cross again. If only Jake had not beeen struck down as he had ... What was the use of wishful thinking?

'Come right in,' smiled Dominie, leading the way. 'Will you have some coffee?'

'I'd love some.' Erica relaxed in the chair Dominie had indicated. 'Have you any news of Jake's condition?'

A quick nod from Dominie and then,

'I phoned earlier and was told that he improved during the night. However, he's still very poorly and they gave no hope of his being out this week.'

Erica's face fell.

'So I won't see him? They're still not allowing visitors?'

'Not yet, but I'm sure they'll let us visit him shortly.

I've to ring again this afternoon. Rohan rang before I did, and then he rang me. They gave him exactly the same information as they gave me.'

'The children must be upset at not being allowed to see their daddy.'

'They are; but being at school will occupy their minds during the day. They stay to lunch, but will be back at half-past three, so you'll still be here when they come home.'

'You don't mind my staying all that time?'

'I enjoy your company, Erica,' she returned, and went off to get the coffee.

They had drunk it, and were strolling in the garden when Erica said, rather awkwardly,

'Your friend Mr de Arden—I gained the impression that he despised me——'

'Oh no!' protested Dominie before the woman could go any further. 'You mustn't think things like that.'

'I have the idea,' continued Erica, by-passing the interruption as though it had not registered, 'that he considers me a designing female whose only interest in Jake is his money.'

Astounded at this outspokenness, Dominie found an excuse for it only when she remembered that Erica had no idea that she was speaking to Rohan's future wife.

'You're quite wrong, Erica.' Dominie had to lie, and yet, as she half-turned her head to note her companion's expression, she knew at once that she wasted her time. However, Erica was now too tactful to carry the matter any further and the conversation turned to Dominie herself, with Erica interestedly asking about her life in England. Obligingly Dominie supplied the information and in turn later heard a little more about Erica's life.

'My husband left me comfortably off,' she said reflectively, 'but I'm not wealthy, by any means. I live in a flat and manage to run a car.' She paused, and bent down to touch with loving fingers the lovely spray orchids cascading over a low wall, their blooms of brilliant pink appearing luminescent as they caught the fierce rays of the sun. A hummingbird hovered intrepidly close to Erica's hand, bringing the whole exotic picture to life. 'Time often hangs, though,' continued Erica, straightening up and allowing her gaze to follow the tiny bird as it flew into a golden candle bush. 'And life becomes a bore. I feel that mine is a useless existence.' She cast Dominie a sideways glance as they began strolling on again, towards the palm-shaded path leading to the swimming-pool. 'You were fortunate in finding a post like this, Dominie, and I think that when I get back home I'll try to find something similar.'

Dominie frowned to herself. To the practical side of her mind it seemed a sheer waste that, with so much to give, Erica must continue to live alone. She cared deeply for Jake; she could make him happy ... With a sigh Dominie braked her wandering thoughts. Rohan was quite right; she was wrong in trying to interfere in something that was not her concern. She must stop thinking about the matter, she told herself sternly, and yet within a few hours she was allowing her imagination full rein once more.

'Jake can have three visitors tomorrow afternoon,' she told Erica, who had rung through to see if there was any news of Jake's condition. 'He's been improving all the time and the doctors say that it was only food poisoning after all but that it had affected him more severely than it does most people. He was dangerously ill for a few hours, we've now been informed, and I must say that I myself believed he was, without being told, and so did Rohan—Mr de Arden. Do you want to see Jake?' Dominie then asked, and to her surprise a rather long silence followed.

'I—I ...' a pause. 'Perhaps I'd better not——'

'Do come,' urged Dominie in quiet persuasive tones. 'I'm sure he'll be glad to see you.'

'It's seven years since last we met.'

'I'll expect you for lunch, Erica. And afterwards we'll all go to the hospital.'

'All?'

'Rohan will drive us there.'

Dominie stared at the receiver for a long while after putting it down, mentally endeavouring to phrase her words so that Rohan would not be vexed. Picking up the receiver again as if it were hot, she then replaced it. Rohan was going to be more than vexed; he was going to be very angry indeed with her. Suddenly the phone rang and she actually jumped.

Rohan was on the line, having rung the hospital a few minutes before she herself had made her call.

'I tried to get you at once, but your phone was engaged. I expect you were ringing the hospital?'

'Yes, and they told me that Jake is improving and that he can have visitors tomorrow——' Dominie stopped to swallow, for her mouth was getting dry. 'I have —have told Erica that she can come with us to the hospital.'

Silence. Had he rung off? wondered Dominie, automatically looking at the receiver in her hand. But no; his voice came over to her, taut and clipped, with that

119

hint of a French accent rather more pronounced than she had ever heard it before.

'What did you say, Dominie?'

'Do you mind very much—taking her with us, I mean?' The evasion brought a swift intake of his breath which was almost like a hiss coming over the line.

'I told you to mind your own business, Dominie! Jake doesn't want to be disturbed by strangers at a time like this. Mrs Edgley's not coming with us. Is that clear?'

'I've told her,' began Dominie almost in tears. 'I can't ring her up now and tell her she can't see Jake.'

'Then I shall! What's her number?'

'I'm not giving it to you,' was Dominie's swift and obstinate reply, a reply that surprised her as much as it surprised Rohan.

'I'll be over in fifteen minutes,' he snapped, and the line went dead.

Dominie had never thought to see Rohan as furious as he was when, on entering the room where she waited, he glowered at her from his superior height, his mouth compressed and his brows knit together in a frown.

'I can't bring myself to tell her——' she began agitatedly, the colour leaving her face. 'Try to understand, Rohan——'

'You had no right to make the promise in the first place,' he rasped, taking a few steps which brought him close up to her. 'Jake's my friend, and I'm not having him pestered by some damned gold-digger at a time like this! He's ill—*ill*! Haven't you got that into your head yet?'

Unconsciously she plucked at the front of her dress.

'Perhaps I sh-shouldn't have been quite so hasty,' she owned, endeavouring to keep her voice steady despite her inner trembling. 'But it's too late to do anything about it now. And—and as for your branding her a gold-digger, that's not at all fair. Erica loves Jake, no matter what you think to the contrary.'

Rohan's eyes glittered and the muscles round his mouth contracted. Dominie lowered her head, her own eyes filling up, and her mouth trembling convulsively.

'If she loved him she'd not dream of intruding at a time like this! In any case, he doesn't love her, so what in the name of Hades is she pushing herself for?'

Dominie started to cry.

'On the surface it does seem—well—silly of her. But you're unable to see things from a woman's view.' Dominie would have elaborated on this, but she was interrupted by the telephone ringing in the hall. Before she could even move, however, Rohan had crossed the room and within seconds she was hearing him say in curt but quietly-controlled tones,

'Mrs Edgley ... Yes, she is ... but is there anything I myself can do for you?'

Dominie reached his side and looked up at him. His expression changed, relaxed in a way that allowed her to breathe a little more freely than she had during the past few minutes. He handed the receiver to her but stood close by, intent upon hearing what was being said.

'Dominie here. Is something wrong, Erica?'

'I've just been telling Mr de Arden that I've changed my mind about visiting Jake tomorrow. It might upset him, having a stranger there—for I am a stranger after all this time.' Erica stopped a moment and Dominie's tear-filled eyes met those of her fiancé.

'We were both a little carried away, I think,' Erica was continuing. 'You were eager that I should see Jake, and so was I. It was only after giving the matter some thought that I came to the conclusion that this isn't quite the right time for me to visit him. He wants his own friends near him, and his children.'

Relief had flooded over Dominie the moment Erica had begun to speak, but she now asked her when she would be coming over to Sunset Lodge.

'You were coming to lunch,' she reminded her, 'and there's nothing to stop your doing so. You can then either stay here until we return from the hospital, or go back to your hotel, whichever you prefer.'

'It's kind of you, Dominie, but I must refuse. I've decided to do a bit more sightseeing because, after all, I shall be leaving St Thomas very soon and I do want to see everything—just in case I never have the chance of coming here again.'

'But——'

'You've been sweet to me—and thank you.'

'Erica—just a minute ... She's hung up on me,' said Dominie in a choked little voice as she allowed Rohan to take the receiver from her and replace it on its rest. 'She's so lonely ... you don't understand.'

'I'm sorry, dear. I realize now that I've misjudged her.' His gentle tones did nothing to assuage her misery. She felt that she and she alone had made Erica desperately unhappy.

'I know now that you were right, but not in the way you think, Rohan.' Lifting her face, she looked into his eyes. 'I did wrong only in that I raised her hopes. You can see that now, can't you?'

'Yes, darling, I can.'

'And there's nothing I can do to help her.' Tears

flowed freely and Rohan took her in his arms, cradling her head against him so that her tears fell on to his shirt. 'I can see her, sitting there in that hotel, on her own, wondering how to pass the time and almost certainly wishing she had never come to St. Thomas.' A sob caught her words and she jerked to a stop. 'Why—why w-won't she come here tomorrow? *Why!*'

'Dearest . . .' Rohan's arms tightened around her. She sensed his remorse and his tender concern that she was unhappy, and weeping. But all she thought of at this moment was that lonely woman, sitting in her hotel room, thinking of what might have been.

'If only I could make her come—just for a few more visits, so that she won't be so alone . . .' Appealingly Dominie looked up at Rohan after pulling away from his hold upon her. 'Do you think I might phone again?'

His lips caressed her pallid cheeks.

'Would you like me to phone, darling?' he asked soothingly, and she started back in surprise.

'Would you? Oh, dearest Rohan, would you really?'

'I would, Dominie. Let me get you a drink first,' and he led her, with an arm about her shoulders, back to the sitting-room where, after pouring her a drink and handing it to her as she settled back against the cushions on the big easy chair, he left her and went into the hall again to telephone Erica.

'Is she coming?' Dominie's breathless question was out even as he re-entered the room and he nodded reassuringly.

'She didn't seem keen at first, but I persuaded her,' he said, looking a trifle grim despite the soft and tender curve of his mouth. 'I'm so sorry, dear. Forgive me for being angry. I was thinking only of Jake, but

123

that's no excuse for hurting you. Say you forgive me, my dear little Dominie.'

She didn't care at all for his humility; it was totally unsuited to his innate superiority and the hint of arrogance that was also an inherited trait.

'There's nothing to forgive. I was wrong in trying to bring them together because, as you said, Jake doesn't love Erica.'

'There is something to forgive,' he argued grimly. 'I've been a brute, and it would serve me right if you were to throw me over——'

'Throw——!' Dominie stared at him. 'I could never do that, no matter what you did to me——' He was looking stern and, realizing he was interested only in her forgiveness, she whispered close to his cheek, 'I forgive you, dearest Rohan—if you must have me say it.' And then she was gathered close into his arms, and she knew the gentleness of him without the mastery, the tender touch of lips that wanted only to soothe away her unhappiness.

Drawing away at last he shook his head in a little action that was half contrite, half disbelieving.

'You've such a tender heart, my Dominie,' he said, a strange gruffness edging his voice. 'And I'm not used to women with tender hearts. I have indeed discovered a treasure.'

She looked swiftly at him, and thought of the women who had caused him pain. There was the young girl who had stolen his father's affections, and in so doing had hurt Rohan by causing hurt to his mother whom he loved. There was Nina, who had injured his pride, if nothing else, by preferring another man, someone with more money, and a title as well. And there had been the woman responsible for his sister's untimely death. It was no wonder that now and then a hardness crept into his make-up, causing him to inflict hurt for which later he was sorry. Lastly, Dominie thought of Sylvia, who was real, whereas to Dominie those others were nebulous people whom she would never even meet. Sylvia had been mercenary, and Rohan had known it, hence the reason for the game he played with her. Yes, mused Dominie as she lifted her face and invited his kiss it was no wonder he became hard and unkind now and then.

Ten days later Jake was back home, pale, and much thinner, but otherwise not too greatly changed by his illness. The children had to be curbed, as in their delight at having their father back at Sunset Lodge they would have given him little peace, desiring that he should come for a swim, or play tennis with them, or take them for a drive in the car. As Jake had to rest for a month Rohan and Dominie took the children out at the week-ends, sometimes to Charlotte Amalie—especially if Dominie had any shopping to do—but more often than not to one of the palm-fringed beaches where they would all swim or play ball on the silver sands, or just laze about under the hot sun. Erica had left the island without having met Jake, but one Sunday, just before Rohan's expected appearance, Susie happened to mention her. Frowning in bewilderment, Jake looked inquiringly at Dominie from his comfortable place on the patio where, in the shade afforded by a vivid magenta bougainvillaea vine, he was relaxing in a low padded garden chair.

'Mrs Edgley ... Are they talking about Erica Edgley?' and when Dominie nodded, 'She's been here?'

'She was on holiday and Rohan and I first met her

when she came up to Rohan at the hotel where we were having lunch. She said she'd like to see you again——' Dominie broke off, flushing slightly as she recalled that Erica had asked about Jake *and his wife*. 'She hadn't heard that you're widowed, and was amazed when Rohan told her.'

'She would be; Doreen was so very young. Erica came here, then, to see me?'

'Yes. She was very upset on learning that you were in hospital.' Dominie was watching his expression intently, but it told her nothing. 'She seemed lonely and I invited her to lunch several times. Once or twice she stayed until after dinner. I didn't think you would mind, Jake?'

'Certainly I didn't mind.' A small silence descended before Jake's voice eventually broke into it. 'I'd have liked to have seen her. It must be seven or eight years since the last time she called here. She was on holiday then, and she just dropped in, knowing I had settled on St Thomas. Doreen was still with me at that time,' he ended reflectively, and a little broodingly.

'She decided against visiting you in hospital, feeling that you wouldn't want to be troubled with a stranger around—— She felt herself to be a stranger, not having seen you for such a long time. Rohan was also of the opinion that it was better that she didn't go to the hospital.'

Jake nodded.

'I don't think I'd have welcomed her there, as I did feel exhausted after the Osbornes' visit, and also after the Meads'. However, I'd have liked to have seen her once I got back home.'

'She had to leave. She came on a package tour.' Jake said nothing. His face was still unreadable, but he

126

seemed to be completely lost in thought ... or was it retrospection? 'She's an exceedingly charming woman,' Dominie ventured hesitantly, and again Jake nodded, but absently. 'She and I took to one another instantly and I was sorry to see her leave.' Still no comment from Jake. 'We're keeping in touch,' added Dominie, and then gave up. Obviously Jake wasn't over interested in the woman of whose love he remained totally unaware.

'Ooh, here's Uncle Rohan!' Susie spoke and on the instant both children were racing towards the car as it slid to a stop by the corner of the house. 'Where are we going today——? Ooh, you've got a picnic basket in the car! Can we go to Coconut Grove and swim and then have our picnic on the sands?'

'That is my idea, Susie.' Rohan frowned at her. 'Go and wash that chocolate from round your mouth.' She lifted a hand, but it was knocked down with a firm but gentle tap. 'I said wash, not wipe!'

'All right—but don't go without me!' and off she ran, back into the house.

'I don't know where she got the chocolate,' said Dominie with a slight frown. 'I washed her face and hands only ten minutes ago in preparation for going out.'

Rohan said, examining Jake's face, which was still a trifle thin and pale,

'How are you today, Jake?'

'I'm improving all the time, thanks, Rohan. I'm beginning to feel like my old self. I suppose having such good friends has helped. I've no anxiety over the kids, which I most certainly would have were it not for you and Dominie.'

She made a protesting gesture.

'I do only what I'm paid for, Jake.'

'And more, my dear. It was my lucky day when I met up with you on that ship.' He paused and glanced from her to Rohan, obviously searching in his mind for the right words. 'I must admit that, before I went away, I had the suspicion that you two might—well—take to one another, and in hospital I began to fret about the possibility of losing Dominie. However, as it's turned out you're just good friends, and I'm selfish enough to be glad of it.' As he was now watching his young daughter with affection as she came running towards him along the length of the patio, he missed the darting glance that passed between Dominie and Rohan—a frowning glance on Rohan's part and a dejected one on Dominie's. She felt flat suddenly and had no enthusiasm for the outing to which she had been so looking forward.

'We'll give him another month,' Rohan was saying an hour later as he and Dominie sat close together on the beach, watching the children paddling on the edge of the shore. 'And then he must be told. I'm not waiting any longer, my dearest heart——' His strong arm enclosed her shoulders and she pressed against his hard brown chest, a strange fear engulfing her. A month ... So much could happen in that time.

CHAPTER EIGHT

WHY was she feeling like this?—unsure of the future, and even of Rohan's continuing to maintain his enthusiasm for the marriage? He was sincere, dependable; he loved her with the same depth and strength

that she loved him, of this Dominie had no doubt ...
so why this obscure but frightening idea that something would prevent their union?

The idea grew with every day that passed, and it
became more and more difficult to hide her depression
from Rohan who with his discerning eye would sometimes notice her pallor and question her in phrases of
anxious endearment.

'It's nothing, darling,' she would say, forcing a smile
in order to clear away the frown that touched his forehead. But one day, her depression having been increased tenfold by Rohan's information that the Fortescues—and their daughter—were coming again to St
Thomas and would be staying at Windward Crest, she
could not keep her fears in check and she said in
answer to his inquiry as to why she wasn't looking too
well, 'I sometimes have a dreadful fear that we won't
ever marry.'

'Won't——?' He stared at her in disbelief. 'My ridiculous child! I'd like to see anything stop us from
marrying!'

So very reassuring, those forcefully-pronounced
words, and for a delicious moment of forgetfulness she
went to him as he stood there, in the secluded part of
the tropical garden in which he and she had been
strolling. He had been telling her about the flowers,
and saying she must add some more of her own once
she was mistress of Windward Crest. His arms opened
intantly and, slipping into them, Dominie lifted her
face, parting her lips as his mouth came down on hers,
so very tenderly and lovingly.

'Haven't I told you, so often, that I adore you?' he
asked presently, still holding her in his arms. 'Haven't
I said that I hate this waiting?' She nodded, remem-

bering his impatience on so many occasions. How could she explain that it was not the waiting which was responsible for the way she felt? She had no other explanation to offer in its place. There was no accounting for her fears which, she kept telling herself, were absurd in the extreme.

'I love you so much,' she whispered close to his lips, thrilling to the expression of love in his eyes, the tender curve of his mouth and the feel of clean cool breath on her face. 'I'm ridiculous, as you say, and I'm determined not to be afraid any more.'

'I shall have to be far more stern with you,' he decided, 'and box your ears when you don't behave as I want you to!'

Shyly she fluttered her lashes.

'I'll behave,' she promised, and this time her laugh was spontaneous, not forced. 'I'll do everything you want me to.'

His amber eyes widened for a fleeting moment before the lines at the sides crinkled, and his lips twitched.

'Everything?' with some considerable amusement. 'Now that is what I call a most tempting offer——'

'Rohan, you're incorrigible!' she laughed.

'That's better,' he approved. 'Keep that happy light in those beautiful eyes—always!'

Dominie promised she would, and for a couple of days did in fact manage to throw off her misgivings and appear the happy bride-to-be. After all, she told herself, she would very soon be able to wear the lovely engagement ring which Rohan had bought her, and once Jake was in the picture, and looking for another nanny, the wedding could be arranged. Meanwhile, though, all unknowing, Jake arranged to have Rohan and the Fortescues over for dinner, and although Rohan deliberately set out to be no more than polite to Sylvia it did seem to Dominie that the girl adopted a possessive manner with him. How did she behave when in his home? Dominie began to wonder, the first pricks of jealousy making themselves felt. The girl and her parents had been at Windward Crest for almost a week; Dominie could not help assuming that Rohan's present attitude of near-indifference towards Sylvia was adopted solely for his fiancée's benefit, since he would not wish to act in a way that Dominie could resent. Was he more friendly with Sylvia at home? It looked very much like it, for otherwise surely the girl would not be so possessively familiar with him.

She was sitting next to him, while Dominie was opposite, and she had to watch the girl fluttering her lashes, and half-turning her pretty head all the time to look at him. She laughed a good deal and he would laugh in response; she whispered to him and he would nod, though absently, Dominie had to admit.

'I'm having another helping of chicken, Jake,' she cooed at her host. 'Oh, look at Rohan's disapproving frown!' Dominie didn't notice any frown; in fact, her fiancé's expression was one of near-boredom. 'He always used to scold me about my eating too much, but you can, Rohan darling, when you're only twenty-one. It's when you're nearing thirty that you have to start being careful,' and she looked slyly at Dominie before laughing and turning to Rohan, expecting him to laugh as well.

Dominie lifted her napkin to her mouth, lowering her head at the same time. She did not think anyone had noticed the subtle barb, simply because she, Dominie, was not 'nearing thirty'. But Sylvia, aware of her age because she herself had once mentioned it to Jake in her hearing, had endeavoured to bring to Rohan's notice the fact that Dominie was several years older than she. On lifting her head at length Dominie met Rohan's gaze. Her lip quivered in spite of herself and he smiled, faintly shaking his head in what could only be described as a little gesture of admonishment. So he knew she was affected by the girl's attitude towards him—and he was anxious to convey the information that, apart from being downright rude to the daughter of a valuable business associate, there was little he could do about it. But Dominie was human, and very much in love; she could be as jealous as the rest ... and she was. And jealousy bred anger which, showing in her expression, brought a sudden dark frown to her fiancé's brow. She glanced down at her plate, then up again, sending him a fluttering look from under her lashes. His mouth was tight, and his eyes had narrowed to slits of anger. Dominie caught up her lower lip between her teeth, biting hard in order to stem the tears which threatened. She heard her fiancé say, with the amused tolerance he had once adopted towards the girl,

'Sylvia, can I pass you the rolls?' and the purring response,

'Thank you very much, dear Rohan. Oh, I do adore their crusty outsides—don't you?'

Stupid creature! thought Dominie to herself, wishing fervently that she could find some excuse for leaving the table.

'Dominie,' said Jake in his quiet good-humoured voice, 'you're not eating very much. What can I pass you?'

'I'll have a little more chicken, please.'

She helped herself from the dish, refusing to glance in Rohan's direction, and he seemed to become more angry than ever because she heard, after a moment, the quick intake of his breath and the unnecessary clatter as his knife and fork were placed on his plate. Dominie looked around the table. Mrs Fortescue was beaming in the direction of her daughter and Rohan; her husband was passing some remark to Jake. Dominie felt alone—out of everything. The food choked her and she wished she had not asked for it. Never had she expected this to be such an unhappy meal for her.

A sigh of relief escaped her when at last they all rose, to move out to the moonlit terrace where coffee and liqueurs were served.

'Take me walking, Rohan, please ...' Sylvia's kittenish request was accompanied by a slipping of her arm through that of Rohan, who was sitting close to her. 'I adore a tropical garden when the moon shines on it! The flowers are all lit up—though not as brightly as when the sun shines on them—and the breeze tonight is so warm and ... heady.'

'The breeze is cool, not warm,' said Jake in some amusement. 'The night would be much less comfortable if it weren't for the breeze, for we've had an exceptionally hot day.'

Sylvia gave an elegant shrug of her shoulders.

'Warm or cool—what does it matter? I want to walk in it. Are you coming, Rohan?'

'Later, Sylvia.'

That should have put Dominie in a better mood, but strangely it didn't. For one thing, she could find no excuse for Rohan's allowing Sylvia's arm to remain were it was, tucked intimately into his, and for another, she felt that even though the engagement must be kept a secret, Rohan could without arousing any suspicions have given his fiancée a little more of his attention. Of course, through her anger at the dinner table she had provoked him, but she was in no mood to make allowances for the subsequent attention he had afforded Sylvia, or reasonably to admit that it was only natural that he should retaliate.

And so when the time arrived for his departure there remained a coolness between them never before existing at a parting. His stiff and formal good night produced in her so choking a sensation that she was quite unable to respond, with the result that he believed she had deliberately snubbed him. Just to add to Dominie's misery it was Sylvia who slipped into the front seat of the car with him, and the last words Dominie heard as Rohan slid the car smoothly off the forecourt were,

'Our stroll, Rohan ... you haven't forgotten? It's not too late, darling ...'

Rohan hadn't put in an appearance for two whole days, nor had he telephoned. Dominie stood by the table on which Jake's phone lay, her fingers pressed into her hair, the palm of her hand as damp as the brow on which it rested. Her fears ... how very real they were now. Not by any stretch of imagination could she visualize her wedding-day. She had lost him, she told herself over and over again even while, glancing at the clock, she was finding yet another excuse for his not phoning. It was eight o'clock, and he dined at that time. Later, when he had settled his guests with their coffee and liqueurs, he would leave them and speak to her, saying he was sorry if she'd been hurt but there had really been nothing he could do about

Sylvia's familiarity, not in her parents' presence. And she, Dominie, would be all contrite, and admit that she had been unreasonably angry and jealous, and she hoped he would forgive her. He would be over early tomorrow, he would then promise, and they would have a wonderful making-up.

But the bell never rang and at half-past nine Dominie had given up hope.

'Is anything wrong?' inquired Jake anxiously as he came up to her in the garden. He had been with the children, having a little talk after Dominie had bathed them and put them to bed. And now he joined Dominie as she stood on the edge of the lawn, staring into space. 'You've not been yourself all day.'

She turned to him, noting his rugged features, more healthy now, and his smile that always had a certain softness about it, as had his eyes a softness about them, even though the brows above were shaggy, giving the impression of austerity.

'I—I don't feel t-too good, Jake,' she admitted and, to her utter dismay, she started to cry.

'Dominie . . .' His arms came around her. 'My dear child——' He broke off, turning, then fell back from Dominie as Sylvia approached, followed by her parents.

'I hope we're not intruding.' Sylvia's silky voice contained a curious note as she glanced from Dominie, whose head was turned away, to Jake who, having made a swift recovery, smiled and stepped forward to where Mrs and Mrs Fortescue had stopped, their eyes questioning and, in the case of Mr Fortescue, faintly apologetic.

'I say, I hope we're not unwelcome, Jake——'

'Indeed no,' was the gracious reply. 'Do come in and

have a drink.'

'As you probably know, Rohan was called away yesterday morning, and as we had an early dinner we thought we'd just stroll along here and say good evening.'

'Rohan was called away?' echoed Dominie, turning swiftly after dabbing at her eyes.

Jake nodded.

'He rang through early yesterday morning to tell me——'

'You never mentioned this,' interrupted Dominie in a sort of breathless haste. 'I—I didn't know.'

Sylvia eyed her arrogantly.

'Was there any special reason why you should know?' she asked.

Dominie was saved an answer by the intervention of Jake, apologizing for not mentioning to her that Rohan had been called away, but adding,

'I didn't think it important. He said he had some urgent business to attend to in New York after having received a phone call from his agents here in St Thomas.' Dismissing the matter of Rohan's absence without the least inkling of the relief he had brought to Dominie, Jake made for the house, accompanied by the Fortescues, while Sylvia lagged behind with Dominie who herself would have kept up with the others but in politeness kept pace with Sylvia. Immediately she saw that the others were out of earshot Sylvia spoke.

'I didn't know that you and Jake were in love. When's the wedding?'

Dominie's mouth tightened.

'Jake and I are not in love.'

'No?' Sylvia was in the shadows cast by the palms,

but Dominie sensed the widening of her eyes. 'You allow men to make love to you, when you're not in love with them! Oh, I know it's the fashion these days, but I never could do anything before marriage.'

Silence, the silence of white-hot fury. Dominie would never know how she prevented herself from slapping the girl's face. Instead she said quiveringly,

'Are you always so disgustingly outspoken, Miss Fortescue?'

Sylvia feigned a sort of injured surprise, appearing to be taken aback.

'What have I said, Miss Worthing? You were in Jake's arms, and he was calling you dear, so I naturally thought——'

'His actual words were, "my dear child"!' snapped Dominie, increasing her pace.

'I naturally thought,' continued Sylvia, ignoring the interruption, 'that there was something between you.'

Choking with fury, Dominie decided on a strategic retreat, before that fury broke all bounds. She slipped through an opening in the hedge and was already in the house when the other four arrived. She went straight up to her room, to be quiet and settle her nerves. Soon her thoughts had switched from the objectionable girl down below to Rohan, and her spirits lightened. He had rung early, perhaps hoping she herself would answer the phone, as Jake was still not getting up until the children had gone off to school. But Jake was up earlier than usual yesterday and must have answered the phone while she was upstairs getting the children ready. Rohan would not ask for her, in case Jake suspected something, but he would naturally take it for granted that Jake would mention the call, and the reason for it. How upset he would be when she told him of these two days of misery she had endured. On second thoughts she decided not to tell him, for there was nothing to be gained by causing him pangs of remorse.

Crossing over to the mirror, she took up a comb and proceeded to put her short curls into order after the touselling they had received from the breeze just now. Her eyes looked back at her from the mirror. They were clearer now, being no longer shadowed with doubts as to why her fiancé had failed to contact her. How long would he be away? If it were to be more than a few days then surely he would write. The thought of a letter brought to mind the one she had received that day from Erica and, sliding forward the drawer of her dressing-table, she took it out, opening the folded sheets and flicking back the first page to read again part of the second.

'How is Jake how? I was so glad to read in your letter that he is improving all the time. I think about him a great deal these days—much more than I did when Doreen was living, for then it hurt, Dominie, so very much. I had no idea they were separated and I used to avoid thoughts of Jake simply because I could not separate him from his wife. I wish I could have met him again, just to see how he looked, after seven years. Perhaps I shall manage another trip some day. You say in your letter that he now knows I was at Sunset Lodge. Give him my regards, please, Dominie, and for yourself—thank you, and God bless.'

Slowly Dominie folded the sheets again and returned them to the drawer, blinking rapidly, just as she had on reading the passage for the first time. As requested she had passed on Erica's message, but apart from a comment to say that it was kind of her Jake had betrayed no interest whatsoever.

With a deep sigh Dominie left her room and joined the others downstairs. On entering the sitting-room she received an anxious, inquiring glance from Jake and smiled at him reassuringly, silently telling him she was all right now. From Mr and Mrs Fortescue she received distinctly odd glances, while that from Sylvia appeared to be one of triumph. Triumph? thought Dominie with a frown. But then she shrugged, dismissing it as unimportant, as she was more interested in learning when Rohan was expected back from his business trip.

She put the question casually to Mr Fortescue, in a quiet voice while Sylvia and her mother were talking to Jake, but Sylvia's ears were sharp and she turned her head, eyes narrowing. But of course she made no comment when her father replied to Dominie's question, although Dominie knew for sure that had they been alone the girl would pertly have asked the reason for Dominie's interest. What a shock she was going to receive when the engagement was announced, thought Dominie, and, because she was only human after all, she could not help but admit that she was going to enjoy the girl's chagrin and discomfiture.

When at length Sylvia and her parents left Jake naturally returned to the subject of Dominie's tears.

'I was feeling off-colour and depressed,' she said, and gave a little deprecating laugh, just for effect. 'It was stupid of me, and I'm perfectly all right now.'

He still looked anxious.

'You're sure? You're not the kind who cries for nothing, Dominie.'

'I—I suppose it was—thoughts,' she murmured, unable to find anything more convincing to say.

'Thoughts?' he frowned, leaning back in his chair

and regarding her through kindly eyes. 'Your brother?'

'Well ... not exactly,' she began, unable to lie outright. But Jake seized on her hesitancy, taking it for granted that she had in fact been troubled by thoughts of Jerry.

'Let me take you out,' he said impulsively. 'Come, put on something pretty and we'll go dancing!'

'It's late——'

'But not too late. Go on, put on that dream of a gown you wore the first time Rohan invited us out.'

'Really, Jake——'

'No argument!'

'One or other of the children might wake.'

'And if they do? There are plenty of servants in the house. Molly will look to them. Off you go, and change.'

'You should be resting.'

'I've rested enough. An hour out will do me good.'

Jake took her to the Virgin Isle where they danced to the steel band and then sat with their drinks and watched the limbo dancers performing with flares in their mouths which ignited the bar under which they had to pass.

'Well, Dominie,' Jake asked as they drove away from the hotel at midnight, 'did that take your mind off things?'

She said, a little wistfully, because she was thinking all at once of Erica,

'You're so kind, Jake ... so very kind.'

She saw him shrug his shoulders. She wondered if he were thinking of his wife, and recalling that she did not consider him kind—or if she did, she had no desire to be the recipient of that kindness.

'It's sweet of you to say so, my dear,' he said at last

140

with a small sigh.

'Do you—do you often feel lonely, Jake?' The question came hesitantly, but she saw at once that he did not resent her familiarity.

'A man on his own does,' he admitted. 'It was grim when the children were in England with their mother. I used to visit my sister in Florida now and then, and she would visit me, but apart from her, I felt I had no one of my own.'

She nodded understandingly, paused a moment and then,

'Have you never thought of marrying again?'

'My wife hasn't been dead very long.'

'But you were separated. You never wanted a divorce——?' She stopped, then added apologetically, 'I shouldn't have asked you that. Tell me to mind my own business, Jake.'

He smiled in the dimness of the car.

'I appreciate your concern, so why should I tell you to mind your own business? No, Dominie, I never thought of divorce, even though I had for a long time been resigned to the fact that there was no hope of a reconciliation.'

'Would you marry now—if you met someone nice?'

He turned his head, to look oddly at her. His expression was revealed in the lights flaring forth from an hotel they were passing and she frowned in puzzlement.

'For companionship, you mean? I'm getting on, my dear.' These words only added to her perplexity; he was only fifty-one, which was still quite young, for a man.

'I don't consider you old, Jake,' she returned gently, and a curious little silence ensued.

141

'You don't?' he said musingly at last. 'You really mean that, Dominie?'

'Most certainly I do. And what you are in years doesn't matter anyway. It's how you look and feel. You look so young—and the way you play with the children—— Indeed you're not old,' she told him with emphasis.

'It's quite true that I don't feel old,' he agreed, and lapsed into a strange silence for a while. 'I shall have to think about it, my dear. Yes, I certainly shall.'

'About remarrying?' she queried eagerly, thoughts racing on ahead to produce a picture of a radiant Erica as a bride.

To her surprise Jake seemed to frown at this eagerness; she gained the impression that he was rather amazed that she should betray it. And to strengthen this impression was the long hesitation that took place before he answered,

'Yes, Dominie, about remarrying.' But he then immediately changed the subject, and to her disappointment Dominie could find no opportunity of bringing in her little piece about Erica, and how attractive she was, and how the children had taken to her.

On their arrival home Molly was still up, but just about to go to bed. They both looked inquiringly at her.

'Geoffrey had the toothache,' she explained before Jake could put his question. 'He's been in dreadful pain, poor mite, and I brought him downstairs and put pepper on it——'

'Pepper?' exclaimed Dominie and Jake together.

'An old-fashioned remedy,' Molly told them gravely, her big eyes rolling in her dusky face. 'He screamed, I must admit, but the heat cured him.'

'It did?' gasped Dominie, amazed.

'Oh yes, it cured him. But he was wide awake and so I sat with him and we looked at pictures.' Molly had met them in the hall and she glanced towards the sitting-room. 'I forgot to put the book away, Mr Harris, but I'll do it before I go to bed——' She broke off and yawned. 'It's the book Mr de Arden brought over for them once, the book with all the pretty pictures of fairies and flowers and animals that his sister made—a scrapbook, he said it was when I asked him. I'll go and put it away,' she said again. 'Mr de Arden said at the time that it must be taken care of.' She would have gone off to the sitting-room, but on seeing her yawn again Jake told her to go to bed.

'I'll see that the book's put away in a safe place. Good night, Molly, and thank you for seeing to Geoffrey.'

'That's all right, Mr Harris—and don't forget if ever you have the toothache: plenty of pepper!'

'Pepper,' whispered Dominie, her amused eyes following Molly up the stairs. 'Poor Geoffrey!'

'He's survived, obviously,' laughed Jake as he led the way into the sitting-room. 'Molly's a case; she has the oddest remedies, but I must admit that nine times out of ten they're effective.'

'I shall have to take Geoffrey to the dentist in the morning. We can't have him in pain.'

Jake stood by the couch and picked up the scrap-book lying there. Dominie stood by the door, not having entered the room and, looking up, Jake said,

'You're for bed?'

'I'm not a bit tired,' she owned, and came into the room.

'Let's have a drink, then.' He poured it, while Dominie sat down on the couch and picked up the book which Jake had put down. Idly she flipped the pages, thinking of the little girl who had pasted in the pictures, so very neatly. Jake took a seat beside her and half-drew the book on to his own knee.

'Fairies and toadstools and gnomes,' he mused. 'How we all loved them when we were small! Fantasy ... and childhood ... No other time in one's life comes up to it, Dominie—for at that time we really and truly *believe*. When we grow older and receive the knocks that disillusion us we cease to believe and there's no more magic left.'

She swallowed. No more magic ... Loving someone was magic.

She flipped more pages, handling the book as if it were something sacred.

'She was so careful. Look at the way she's cut round these flowers.'

Jake nodded, and flipped another page.

'Babes in the Wood. She's cut round every leaf separately, and almost covered the children with them.'

'And more leaves falling from the tree.' Sadness swept through Dominie and she had no wish to see any more of the child's work. But Jake was turning page after page until the end was reached. And there, in the back, was a large envelope.

'What's this? Cuttings she never got round to pasting in, I expect.' Jake lifted the flap and shook the contents on to the open book. 'No, these are nothing to do with the book ... but they are to do with Alicia. This is her picture. She was about sixteen.' He held out the snapshot and Dominie looked at the sweet young face of her fiancé's sister.

'She was ... beautiful,' breathed Dominie, sadness

sweeping through her again. 'And this is her about a year later, I should think?' She picked up another snapshot from the book. 'It's taken at Windward Crest.'

'That's right. She's on the terrace—at the far end; it's a bit different now, as Rohan's had more bushes put in.'

He found another snapshot and handed it to Dominie, while he idly leafed through cuttings from a school magazine reporting on the skill of Alicia at games and swimming. One cutting carried a picture of a group of schoolgirls dressed in medieval costume.

'It mentions here how good an actress she was,' commented Jake, going on to say that this cutting was not from the school magazine but from the local newspaper. 'Now what the devil's this supposed to be?' he said suddenly, and held the snapshot out for Dominie to see.

'This ...?' She frowned and took it from him. 'I know where this is,' she murmured, puzzled that it should be here, among these papers which Rohan had saved. 'It's a snap of a place not far from where I used to live. What on earth could he want with it? There's no one on it—and the view is scarcely one on which you'd waste a film.' She shook her head, absently fingering a corner where the impress of a paper-clip gave evidence that something had been attached to the snapshot at one time. 'How very strange! Imagine Rohan knowing this place.' Turning the snapshot over, she saw, written in a bold hand, the names of the main road and the minor road leading on to it, with its halt sign clear and prominent.

'I remember now,' Jake was saying as he took the snapshot from her to scan it again. 'This is the spot where the accident occurred. The man who witnessed

145

it took this the following morning and posted it to Rohan, having got his address from the hospital to which Rohan took his sister, not at that time realising she was dead. The man seemed to think he was helping Rohan, that through this he might be able to do something about finding the woman, but of course it was ridiculous. In any case, Rohan was too grief-stricken to bother about a search at that time, especially when he had absolutely nothing on which to go. Apparently the woman put her lights off, so it was impossible to see her number. Rohan shouldn't keep this,' added Jake almost angrily. 'What good does such a reminder do?' He was frowning at the words on the back of the snapshot, lapsing into silence as he stared at them.

Dominie was also frowning, but unconsciously. As Jake had begun to speak strange tingles—almost imperceptible at first—swept along her spine. The sensation began slowly to take a more palpable form and she found herself shivering. Memory was returning . . . Suddenly a numbness gripped her legs and her hands felt as if ice had touched them. Jake was speaking again, saying he would very much like to throw away the snapshot, as it could only hurt Rohan every time it came to light. Turning his head as he talked, he gave a start on seeing Dominie's expression.

'What on earth's wrong with you?' he exclaimed. 'You look as if you've seen a ghost!'

Dominie just stared, unable to speak, while every nerve in her body rioted and her heart thudded madly against her ribs. She closed her eyes, and then she heard herself speaking, disjointedly, huskily, and in tones no louder than a whisper.

'I—I have something to tell you . . .' She had realized

146

she was mumbling incoherently and now she endeavoured to be more articulate. 'But first, Jake, you must make me a solemn promise that you will never, under any circumstances, repeat what you hear to Rohan?'

'Dominie ... What is this all about? You're so white——'

'The promise, Jake,' she pleaded, driven by some urgent force to relate to someone what had happened.

'Of course I promise.'

'You remember my telling you about Jerry, and about my driving home afterwards?' Jake nodded and she continued, 'I was dreadfully ill with shock, and during that drive home I had a complete blank in my memory. All I could recall was a screech of brakes, and I've felt, all this time, that something important happened during those few blank moments.' She stopped, aware of Jake's deep puzzlement. An agonizing lump had risen in her throat and she swallowed several times in order to remove it. Her voice was no more than a whisper when at length she was able to speak. 'I was the woman responsible for the accident that killed Rohan's sister.'

'You——!' Jake stared uncomprehendingly. 'What are you talking about?'

'It all fits,' she told him, black despair in her voice. 'I always knew it would come back to me some time, and now it has, owing to my seeing that snapshot. I know exactly what happened during those few lost minutes. I came out of the side road without stopping. I heard the dreadful screech of brakes...' Dazedly she moved her head from side to side, trying to concentrate. 'I always thought they were my own brakes, but I now know they were Rohan's. I stopped and a man tapped on the window. When I let it down he put his head inside the car and said I was—was drunk . . .' Again she tailed off, frowning heavily. 'He said something else first. I can't recall what it was——' She shook her head. 'It doesn't matter; it's not important. I remember mumbling about Jerry,' she went on as Jake would have interrupted, 'because his face was before me all the time——' She shuddered violently at the picture and comfortingly Jake took her cold hands in his. 'I scarcely knew what I was doing or saying, but I do remember saying over and over again that Jerry was dead, that the lorry had killed him. Don't you see, Jake, how it all fits?'

'I'm damned if I do,' he exploded after an incredulous silence. 'You were never drunk in charge of a car! The man said he smelled whisky, or some spirit. You never touch spirits!'

Dominie explained about the spilled brandy, going on to say that the smell of this, added to the fact that she was probably mumbling incoherently, would without doubt give the man the impression that she was drunk in charge of the car.

'I caused the accident,' she whispered in an anguished voice. 'It does fit, Jake, no matter what you say.'

He looked at her, frowning heavily. Then he shook his head, as if determined to throw off any doubts she had managed to put into his mind.

'You never caused that accident,' he declared. 'I'm absolutely sure of it.'

'You're kind, Jake, but it isn't any use. I know I came out of that road——'

'This particular road,' he cut in, taking up the snapshot again and tapping it almost savagely. 'You actually recall coming out here?'

She hesitated, her eyes flickering uncertainly.

'It must have been that road——'

'Was it! Never mind about the "must have been". Let's keep to facts.'

'This is the road I'd use, Jake. A few hundred yards along the other road—the one I came into—is the junction with the dual carriageway, and I remembered everything from the time I reached it.'

Jake did not speak for a moment; he was in one of his familiar moods of thoughtful silence.

'You've just said that you remember *exactly* what happened during those lost few moments,' he said at last, turning his head to look straight into her eyes. 'But there's a good deal still missing as far as I can see. You haven't yet mentioned the accident itself. Did you see it?'

Dominie shook her head.

'I wouldn't, would I? You see, I drove on a little way—the witness said this——'

'Forget the witness,' Jake cut in roughly. 'Do you yourself remember driving on after you heard this loud application of brakes?'

She nodded, but frowned to herself.

'Y-yes...'

'You don't seem very sure?'

'I am sure, Jake,' she said quickly, but again she frowned inwardly. She had not quite got the full picture, she realized. However, she knew for sure that she had caused the accident. It had occurred at a point where she would enter the main road; there was the witness who smelled the alcohol; he said the woman driver had mumbled incoherently, and Dominie knew that she had done this. In fact, she clearly recalled muttering all the way home—repeating that Jerry was dead. 'Yes,' she continued thoughtfully, 'I did drive on. So I wouldn't see the accident because it was behind me. The night was very dark,' she added, 'and there were no street lights, as it was a country lane.' Jake gave a sigh and Dominie went on to point out that it would be a very strange coincidence if there was another woman driver, smelling of drink, and coming out of the side road without stopping, at about the same time as Dominie herself was doing so. 'It was me,' she ended with conviction. 'It's quite impossible that it could have been another woman.'

After a long silence Jake began to nod, biting his lip hard.

'You can't remember what the man said to you?' he inquired, rather in the manner of someone clutching at a straw.

'No, but as I said, it isn't important. I do clearly remember that he said I was drunk, and in such a contemptuous voice.'

'I'm not at all convinced that you have the road right,' Jake then said with a sort of dogged persistence, even while, on noting his haggard expression, it was clear to Dominie that he had accepted the fact of her being responsible for the accident.

'It definitely was the road, Jake. I would have to come that way from the mortuary——'

'Along a country lane?'

She gave a small impatient gesture with her hand.

'My home was in the suburbs, and you have to use that particular road to get to and from the town. It's a sort of legacy from the past. There's still a farm on one side of it.'

'I can't think you were responsible,' said Jake in a hoarse voice. 'There *must* be some mistake!'

'I knew those lost moments would return one day,' she murmured, ignoring Jake's well-meaning protest. Heaving a great sigh, she began trembling from head to foot as the stark reality of her situation struck her forcibly. She was the one responsible for the death of Rohan's sister, the woman he hated most in all the world. 'Rohan,' she cried in a strangled voice. 'Oh, my dearest, forgive me!'

'My dearest...?' Jake stared, but instantly put this from him as, noticing how she trembled, he sprang to his feet and drew her to him. Her face was like parchment, her eyes glazed. 'There *is* some mistake!' he almost shouted, but his voice betrayed his doubt.

'There's no mistake——' Dominie buried her face in his coat and wept. 'No mistake ... I killed Alicia.'

CHAPTER NINE

JAKE paced the floor, inwardly groaning with exasperation.

'You can't throw him over!' Swinging round, he came back to where Dominie was sitting on the couch, her head in her hands. 'I refuse to remain silent and let you ruin both your lives!' The forceful manner was unfamiliar to Dominie, who hitherto had seen Jake only in a gentle mood.

'You should go to bed,' she told him listlessly. 'This isn't good for you.' She glanced at the clock. 'It's past two,' she added, and put her head in her hands again. She was drained, but there was a determination in her that nothing would move. Her head had begun to throb violently the moment enlightenment dawned, and the continued pain was dulling her senses. 'Please go to bed——'

'You can marry him without telling him,' almost shouted Jake. 'How is he ever to learn that it was you?'

She looked up.

''We've been into all this, Jake. I can't carry a weight like that all my life. There should be no secrets between husband and wife. Each should know everything about the other—everything of importance, that is.'

Jake drew an angry breath and turned away from her, into the centre of the room, where he stood for a long moment, in brooding wrathful silence.

'You say you can't remain silent if you're married, yet you're not willing to come out with the whole story now. Why not?' he demanded, twisting his large body so that he faced her. 'What harm can you do by going to him and putting the facts before him? Why can't you let *him* decide whether or not there's to be a marriage?'

'Because I don't want him ever to know that it was I who killed his sister. I shall give him up for the reason which I've already explained to you.'

'You'll crucify him! He's been jilted once——'

'No, Jake, you said yourself that there was no actual engagement.'

'You have so many answers, Dominie,' said Jake in a slightly quieter tone. 'If only I hadn't opened that damned book,' he added, glaring at it as it lay on the small table by the window. 'If only you yourself had never learned the truth!'

'It would have come back to me some time, when we were married and I had been glancing through the book, as I most surely would have done, one day when I came across it.'

'When you were married, yes. Far better then than now!'

Dominie shook her head, wincing as a stabbing pain shot out from the slightly duller agony that seared her head and eyes.

'No, Jake; it's better that revelation came before we were married. I shall at least have the consolation that he'll never hate me for killing his sister, because, this way, he won't ever know that I killed her.'

'He'll hate you for throwing him over!'

Her lips quivered.

'True ... but this won't hurt either of us as much as if he hated me for cutting short that lovely girl's life.'

Jake sat down on a chair opposite to her and, leaning forward, took both her hands in his.

'Dominie, my child, for God's sake look at this situation logically,' he begged, his whole manner changing as the familiar gentleness reasserted itself. 'Rohan will understand, if you explain how it was. You came from the mortuary, having undergone the terrible ordeal of having to identify your brother. You couldn't think or see or act—you were numbed with grief. Rohan's bound to understand.'

She shook her head, and drew her hands from his.

'He might try to understand, because he loves me and wants to marry me, but what about the future? Alicia's birthday, the date of her death, other memories that inevitably must come to him over the years? He'll look at me then and remember that it was I who was responsible for her death ... and he'll come to hate me, Jake,' she whispered convulsively, clenching her hands till the fingernails dug painfully into the palms.

'I couldn't bear that——' She shook her head. 'The way I've chosen is best, for us both.' Jake merely tightened his mouth in a little gesture of frustration and Dominie continued, 'You say I couldn't think or act. This was true, and therefore, it was criminal of me to attempt to drive the car.'

'Nonsense! It was because of the way you were that you did attempt to drive. Had you been able to think you'd have known that you weren't in a fit condition to do so. And another thing: you weren't to blame anyway. Someone at the police mortuary should have seen your condition, and taken you home. It was criminal of *them* to let you go off on your own.'

Dominie moved impatiently.

'I alone am to blame——'

'I won't have that!—and neither will Rohan. I'm telling him, Dominie.'

'You won't! You promised.'

'Before you began. You made me promise without my knowing what you were about to say. I don't now consider myself held to that promise, not after what I've learned.'

Dominie looked into his eyes.

'I shall never speak to you again if you break your word, Jake,' she warned him, but in gentle tones. 'It's my profound wish that Rohan shall never know that I killed Alicia——'

'Will you stop using that word! You didn't kill her!'

'Then who did?' Dominie's face was white, and devoid of expression. Her heart within her seemed dead. That she of all people should be the one responsible for Alicia's death, she thought, irony twisting her mouth. Fate was diabolically cruel.

'Rohan will understand,' repeated Jake stubbornly, bypassing her question, for he could find no answer to it, obviously. That he wished he could was clearly portrayed on his drawn and anxious face, and Dominie knew a fleeting moment of warmth. But she said, in tones of utter despair,

'He'll never be given the opportunity of understanding. I mean what I say, Jake; he's to remain in ignorance of the fact that it was I who was driving that car.'

Jake stood up; he was restless and tired. She asked him again to go to bed.

'You've been ill,' she reminded him, but he cut her short with an impatient lift of his hand.

'I'm not going to bed until I know what your intentions are.'

'I've told you; I'm giving him up and leaving St. Thomas.'

'What about me, and the children?'

She spread her hands, saying he would have lost her anyway.

'As I've mentioned, Rohan was unwilling to prolong our engagement and he intended telling you about us as soon as he considered you were well enough to begin looking round for someone else. I'll stay until you get someone, Jake.' Even in the midst of her misery she could think of Erica and she added, 'Tomorrow, when we're less tired, we'll talk about it. I think I know someone who might like to come and care for the children.'

Jake brushed that off, not having taken much notice of what Dominie was saying, because his mind was otherwise occupied.

'I can't see Rohan accepting your reason for giving

him up,' he said after a long while. 'From what you've told me he's just about as much in love as any man can be, and he knows that you feel the same about him, so he's going to start thinking when, just like that, you tell him it's all off.'

Dominie made no reply for a few minutes as she mused on the way in which she could tackle the problem of ending the engagement with as much speed as possible. For if she became entangled in an argument she must surely burst into tears and blurt out the whole. This she was determined to avoid. Rohan must never ever learn the truth about the accident that robbed Alicia of her life.

'As I told you, Jake,' she said at last, 'Rohan and I weren't too friendly when he left the other evening. He knew I was angry because of the way he was with Sylvia——'

'You said it was the way Sylvia was with him,' Jake interrupted to remind her. 'Also, you admitted that your anger was unreasonable, quite misplaced, directed at Rohan when he himself had done nothing.'

'That's true, I did say so, and I admit I was wrong in being angry with him. But that isn't important—except that it helps me in my purpose, of course.' How calm she sounded! She was talking about ending her engagement just as if it didn't matter. But she was numbed inside and could not feel. Tomorrow her heart would be wrenched right out of her by the pain of the parting she intended to bring about. 'He was also angry,' she continued on noticing Jake's attitude of waiting. 'He was angry with me for being unreasonable. And so he was cool and unfriendly when he said goodnight.'

'I never noticed,' Jake cut in, and Dominie then

pointed out that he would not notice, simply because at that time he had no knowledge of the engagement and, therefore, would not be looking for a sign of affection in Rohan's goodnight.

'I was too upset to answer him,' she went on, her mouth trembling at the memory. 'I was hurt and contrite and—oh, I felt awful, Jake! And as I failed to answer him he would naturally conclude that I'd done it on purpose, because I was still angry. Then when he didn't call or phone I was frantic that he didn't want anything more to do with me——'

'That was my fault,' interrupted Jake with a frown. 'He phoned me and naturally expected me to mention the call to you, telling you the reason for it——' He broke off, his frown deepening. 'You know,' he went on thoughtfully, 'I do seem to recollect that he asked me to mention to you that he was called away ... yes, I'm sure he did.' Jake looked at her through almost anguished eyes. 'Why didn't I remember? I expect I attached no particular importance to the message.'

'Of course you wouldn't,' she agreed, 'not being in the picture regarding our relationship.'

'No ...' Again he became thoughtful. 'This evening on the way home——' He glanced at the clock automatically. 'Last evening,' he amended, 'when you spoke of my remarrying I actually believed you were—were making a subtle proposal to me——' He broke off, uttering an impatient exclamation. 'What made me say that? It's nothing to do with this business of your intention of breaking your engagement.'

But Dominie was diverted, having been utterly taken aback by his admission.

'I was thinking of Erica,' she told him at last.

'Erica?—and me?'

'She loves you, Jake,' responded Dominie quietly, feeling sure that Erica would not mind at all that she was telling Jake this. 'She's loved you for a very long time.'

A profound silence followed, with Jake lost in reflection and Dominie watching him closely for any signs of emotion.

'Erica...' he breathed, and after another pause, 'What did she look like?'

'She's slim and dainty—and exceedingly pretty. She came here several times, as I told you. She was lonely, Jake.'

He looked at her, then his eyes fell on the scrapbook and he said, returning his gaze to her,

'The children? How did she get along with them?'

'They liked her enormously; she was happy when reading to them or playing with them. They all got along fine together.'

Jake's eyes were still fixed on Dominie's white face. He said gently,

'In the midst of your own heartache you can spare a thought for others. No wonder Rohan loves you. You can't leave him, Dominie,' he added with a slight lift to his tone. But she was shaking her head and unconsciously he spread his hands in a helpless gesture.

'To return to Rohan and me,' she said. 'The fact that he believed me to have snubbed him by not bidding him goodnight has helped the situation. He'll think I'm moody and unpredictable. So when I quarrel with him over his not letting me know he was going away he'll not be too surprised.'

Jake was staring at her in disbelief.

'Do you really believe that he's going to let you go as easily as all that? Oh, I know you've explained about the method you're intending to adopt, but I said then and I say now, that Rohan isn't going to let you go. He'll suspect something beneath this weak and totally unconvincing excuse for throwing him over—and, knowing Rohan as I do, I can say without any doubt at all that he'll get the truth from you, even if he has to resort to coercion. So watch your step, Dominie; Rohan isn't an ordinary man—not a softie like me. You haven't seen the other side of his character, but if you do you'll not forget it in a hurry.'

Dominie was afraid, now that the time had come to meet Rohan, and tell him the engagement was ended. And she decided in one moment of panic to leave the island by the first available plane. But that idea was soon crushed. She could never leave Jake in the lurch. He might eventually send for Erica, but that was in the future, and Dominie's problem was concerned with the present. She told Jake of her fear when, immediately on his arrival at Windward Crest, Rohan telephoned to say he was coming over in about half an hour's time.

'Obviously you're afraid,' returned Jake, shaking his head at her. 'And it's all so unnecessary. Rohan loves you, and love can overlook anything.'

'Not anything, Jake. As I said, the time will come when he'll hate me——'

'Rubbish!'

'I'm giving him up,' she said quietly and, uttering a deep sigh, Jake left her, standing there, on the terrace, among the flowers, a forlorn figure whose eyes were pricking with unshed tears and whose heart seemed to be seared right in two.

She glanced towards the drive as the car came along

it, the fact that Rohan had been too impatient to walk only adding to her unhappiness. He was so eager to see her, to make up their little difference of the other night ... to take her in his arms and claim her eager lips.

White-faced and trembling, she began to walk to a secluded bower, first making sure he had seen her. He followed after getting from the car.

'Dominie,' he said huskily on reaching her. 'My girl ... I'm sorry if you were hurt.' His inviting arms were spread and she had to exert all her force to control her legs, to prevent them from carrying her the couple of yards which separated her from the man she loved—the only man she would ever love. He was sorry ... The apology registered, and it hurt excruciatingly that she was unable to tell him from the depths of her contrite heart that it was she who should apologize, as the fault had been all hers. But the apology served another purpose and, looking at him up and down, she said,

'So you should be, Rohan! Your conduct was disgraceful. And you didn't even phone me to say you were sorry—you just went off, not caring how I felt.' She stopped, choked with misery as she saw his outstretched arms fall to his sides, and his face go pale beneath its tan. 'If you treat me like that now, then what would it be like if we were married?' She swept him another contemptuous glance. 'I'm not willing to take the risk,' she added on a note of finality, half-turning from him in disdain. 'Our engagement's off, and—and here is your ring.' She held it out, not daring to glance at him as he stood there, to one side of her, bereft of speech.

He managed to speak at last, his voice faintly harsh,

but disbelieving also, and edged with hurt.

'Are you out of your mind? Are you fully aware of what you're saying?' He seemed dazed; his arrogant air that was almost always in evidence was replaced by bewilderment, and those wide straight shoulders sagged a little. Emotion swelled within her, pressing against heart and nerves in its effort to escape in a flood of tears and words of tender love. How could she remain here, distanced from him and the arms in whose embrace she could find herself, if only she would unprison her desires? She closed her fingers round the ring which he had made no move to take, and an uncontrolled step took her one pace nearer to her beloved. But then she stopped, that terrible memory slashing through her mind again, the memory that she was the woman responsible for his sister's death. No, she told herself in one final resolve to adhere to her plan, there could be no future for Rohan and herself ... not with a shadow like that looming between them for the rest of their lives together. His hatred would begin as a little thing—a germ fertilized by a small tiff, perhaps. And it would grow, nourished by memories, as she had explained to Jake, and in the end Rohan would be unable to hold his hatred in check and he would reveal it to her in all sorts of ways. Better to end it now, when there would be the kind of hatred that would through the years dilute itself to mere dislike, and eventually to nothing more than indifference and, in the end, complete forgetfulness. Yes, Rohan would forget her; men were like that. He would have the odd affair, she felt sure, having experienced his ardour on more than one occasion. And some time, when he became tired of affairs he might look around for someone to marry——

'Dominie! I've spoken to you! Answer me—don't stand there looking superior and arrogant. Answer me, I say!' Fury had now risen, as Dominie knew it would, and she heard her voice tremble when she spoke.

'I've said all there is to say. I have no intention of marrying you——' The words were brought to a shuddering stop as, seizing her by the arms, Rohan shook her until she felt that every bone in her body was broken. 'Rohan . . . oh, please don't!'

'What is it all about?' he snarled, his anger-contorted face above her, his amber eyes lit with the flame of undiluted wrath. 'You love me—I'm sure of it! What's happened? By heaven, Dominie, I'll not be responsible for my actions if you don't come out with an explanation—immediately!' He flung her from him and she fell back against a tree, the ring slipping from her nerveless fingers to roll away into a crevice in the stonework flooring of the bower.

'I d-don't love you,' she managed, putting her arms behind her back so that he should not be able to grasp them again. The action seemed to sober him a little and the twist on his face disappeared. 'I can't marry you, Rohan.'

'Can't? he echoed swiftly, his eyes intent and deeply searching. '*Can't*, Dominie?'

She realized her mistake, and immediately set out to rectify it.

'I can't run the risk of being treated badly——'

'Badly?' he exclaimed, staring at her in amazement.

'You certainly treated me dreadfully the other evening,' she snapped, lifting her head and glaring at him. 'Flirting with Sylvia! What sort of life can I expect with a man who flirts *before* his marriage—flirts right in front of his fiancée's eyes! How humiliated I should have been had our engagement not been a secret!' She stopped. Would he kill her? she wondered for one wild moment of terror as she watched the crimson tinge of colour creep into the tan of his cheeks and the almost satanic twist of fury return to his mouth.

'I asked you for an explanation,' he thundered, taking a step which brought him close again. '*What's happened!*'

She said through whitened lips,

'I see that you're so pompous, so very sure of your attractions, that it's quite impossible for you to take in the fact that you're being jilted. But that is the case, and you have no alternative than to accept it.' Would that convince him? she wondered in a sort of panic. Jake had warned her that Rohan would not be thrown over so easily. He had also warned her of this other side of Rohan's nature, but although she had expected anger, and braced herself to receive it, never in her wildest imaginings could she have visualized a fury like this. He was like a fiend, his handsome face a contortion of almost evil lines. And those hands ... the long hands, with sensitive fingers, strong and brown ... They were opening and closing spasmodically ... as if they were itching to grasp a throat—her throat—and press the life out of its owner. Dominie swallowed, removing saliva collecting in her mouth. If only she had not chosen this secluded place ... Her thoughts trailed off; too late to think of that now. Rohan's face had become even more evil, but the hands were still and his shoulders had straightened, resuming their more familiar aspect of arrogance.

'That's your last word?' he asked at last in tones of terrible harshness. 'You have nothing more to say?'

'Nothing.' The one word was no more than a whisper, but he heard it and, turning, made to leave the bower. 'Your ring,' she said, feeling somehow that she must not on any account allow him to go without it. The return of it would finalize the separation—immutably. Bending, she picked it up, but in her nervousness she let it fall again, this time into the stony earth round the bole of a tree. As she bent again to retrieve it she saw a perfectly-shod foot come close to her hand and as she watched, the lovely ring was ground into the soil between the protruding roots of the tree.

The next moment she was alone, the ring in her hand, the gold twisted but the diamond glittering in the sun. Dominie's tears flowed to mingle with the soil adhering to the setting, and the mud thus made trickled through her fingers. She wiped them on her dress, unthinkingly and, dropping the ring into her pocket, she left the bower and walked slowly back to the house.

Jake was waiting, his face drawn and haggard.

'You did it, then. I knew by the way Rohan drove off. He didn't come in, of course,' he added, shaking his head. 'Dominie, how could you?'

'There was no other way, Jake. It wouldn't have worked out.'

'You've broken him in two.'

'He'll forget, in time.'

'I don't profess to know just how deeply he loved you, Dominie, but I do know that Rohan would have to be able to give his all before he'd ask a woman to be his wife.'

Her face puckered at this.

'I know,' she whispered, and the next moment she was in Jake's arms, weeping against his breast.

'Hush ... hush, child. Why—oh, why don't you have a little sense!'

He dried her tears, then held her to him again. And it was at that moment that Rohan returned, coming quietly on to the patio after leaving his car at the end of the drive. He stood in the open window and watched the swift drawing apart of Jake and Dominie.

'So this is how it is,' he said, his voice like a whiplash despite its quietness. 'Sylvia told me there was something between you, but I didn't believe her when she said she saw you together. I've now seen you for myself.' Scornfully he flicked them in turn. 'Forgive me for intruding,' he said, and went back the way he had come.

'Rohan——!' called Jake, but he walked straight on, without even turning his head. 'What a damnable situation!'

'I'm terribly sorry, Jake. What a mess I've made of everything,' she cried in anguish. 'I've come between you and Rohan——'

'That'll soon be put right, so don't add to your heartache by unnecessary self-blame.' He stopped and listened to the sound of Rohan's car as the engine caught. 'He came back to try again,' said Jake when the engine presently purred away to silence. 'He wasn't willing to accept your explanation. I warned you it would be like that.'

She closed her eyes tightly, but the tears trickled from beneath her lashes. Rohan had come back ... He would have persisted until her defence had cracked. Yes, she knew it without any measure of doubt. Had Rohan found her alone he would not have left until the whole story was out.

'You're going to tell him the truth, straight away?'

Dominie imagined Jake would waste no time in getting Rohan on the telephone, once he had estimated he would have arrived back home.

'The truth?'

'I mean about us—you and me.'

'Of course. I'm not adding to his misery by allowing him to harbour the mistaken belief that I'm the reason for your breaking the engagement.'

Dominie hesitated.

'If you could wait, just a little while . . .?'

'Wait?' he frowned. 'Wait for what?' Clearly he was impatient with her, and she could not blame him.

'I do realize that you're anxious to disillusion him as regards any conclusions he has reached about you and me. But if you tell him the truth now he's bound to come here to see me immediately.'

Jake looked hard at her, into those misted eyes that were shadowed with pain.

'And you feel that if he does come back you'll not be able to maintain your present attitude?'

She nodded and admitted that this was true.

'He might, as you said, coerce me into telling him the truth.'

'It amazes me that he hasn't already done that.'

Automatically Dominie fingered her arms, wondering if she would see bruises when she took off her blouse.

'He—he was far from gentle,' she owned, her lips quivering.

Jake's eyes softened.

'I sincerely wish I'd never been rash enough to make that promise,' he said, but on noting her expression he went on to assure her that he would never break it.

'And you'll wait, just a little while, before telling

him that there's nothing between you and me?'

'He's my very good friend. Dominie. I can't allow him to be hurt any more than he is. Have you thought of the blow to his pride—the knowledge that you prefer an old man with two children to him?'

'I've thought of that, yes, but I'd feel safer if you do allow him to think it, just until I get away from here.' It escaped her that the polite response to Jake's words would be an instant denial that he was old; and by the time it did strike her the appropriate moment of voicing the denial had passed.

'Until you get away from here,' repeated Jake, looking hard at her. 'Hasn't it occurred to you that, once Rohan is put in possession of the truth regarding you and me, he's very likely to follow you to England and demand the very explanation that you're fearing at the present time?'

'It has occurred to me,' she owned, but went on to say that it was most unlikely that Rohan would do so. 'The very fact of my leaving here will be proof and enough that I want nothing more to do with him. Rohan would therefore never lower his pride and come and beg me to take him back.'

Jake was deep in reflection, as he so often was, and although Dominie did wonder what he could be pondering so carefully at a time like this, she fell silent and waited patiently for him to make up his mind about her request. Suddenly she saw his eyes widen, then his lids came down as he noticed her gaze fixed on his face.

'All right,' he agreed with a lack of reluctance that amazed her. 'Yes, Dominie, I'll keep quiet until you've left the island.'

She eyed him with suspicion.

'You don't seem to mind that I'm leaving?'

'Of course I mind,' he retorted roughly. 'But as you're quite determined to do so there's no point in my wasting time in trying to prevent you. You're throwing Rohan over and so obviously you want to avoid the inevitable meeting up with him which would occur were you to remain on the island.'

Dominie was still suspicious. There was something about Jake that she did not understand.

'And when I've left—you won't give away my secret to Rohan? Promise, Jake, for he must never know that I caused that accident.'

Jake looked unflinchingly into her eyes.

'I make you a solemn promise that I shall never mention a word of what I know, to Rohan.'

'Thank you,' she said with relief. 'I—I never really believed you'd let me down.' She managed a fluttering smile and Jake responded.

'I have work to do,' he said abruptly as Dominie would have spoken again. 'Excuse me, dear. I'll be in my study for about an hour.'

'No more,' she warned, 'or I shall be there to bring you out. You're still supposed to be resting.'

Nodding, he left her. She stared at the closed door and frowned.

There was still something about Jake that she did not understand.

CHAPTER TEN

WITHIN a week Dominie was ready to leave St Thomas. Jake had seemed almost eager for her to go, a circumstance which was puzzling in the extreme, and one which naturally hurt her despite the fact of her wishing to leave as soon as possible.

'I've sent a cable to Erica,' he told her only a few hours after Rohan's unforgettable visit. 'I've asked her to take over the post of nanny to the children.'

'She'll accept it,' Dominie assured him, and she was right. Erica sent an air-mail letter saying she was arranging to lease her flat and store her car, and then she would be right over. She wrote another letter to Dominie, asking why she was leaving her job, but for the present Dominie left the letter unanswered.

'She says she'll come for a six-month trial,' Jake told Dominie. 'I hope we'll all get along all right.'

'I'm sure you will.' Six months ... Surely Jake would fall in love long before the end of that time.

'You needn't wait until she arrives,' said Jake, seeming deliberately to avoid her eyes. 'Molly can manage for a couple of weeks.'

'Thank you, Jake.' She supposed one of the reasons for Jake's urgency was that he desired to let Rohan know as soon as possible that there was nothing between him and Dominie. Another reason could be that he was finding it a strain to keep her departure secret from his friends. His embarrassment had been plain a couple of days after her decision was made when, on bumping into the Osbornes when he and Dominie were shopping in Charlotte Amalie, Mrs Osborne had invited them to a barbecue which was being held in their grounds a fortnight later. Unable to say that Dominie was returning to England, owing to the certainty that this would swiftly get to Rohan's ears, Jake had thanked Mrs Osborne for the invitation and said that he and Dominie would be there.

'When I've left,' said Dominie apologetically when the Osbornes had gone, 'you can say that I was called away urgently owing to a personal problem having cropped up at home.'

Jake had merely nodded, but looked harassed. Feeling guilty, Dominie had thanked him for his patience and co-operation, but once again received no response.

'Can I take you out to dinner tomorrow evening?' Jake asked two days before her departure. 'We'll not stay out late, seeing that you have to be away so early on the following morning.'

She agreed and they went to Bluebeard's Castle which, Dominie soon realized, was not a good choice, since it brought back memories of the several occasions when she had lunched and dined there with Rohan. However, she tried to look bright, and to eat her food, for Jake's benefit, and she felt that she had succeeded, for she even managed to laugh at something he had said. When the meal was over they went outside for a while, looking down over the beautiful harbour of Charlotte Amalie, with its twinkling lights sweeping back from the shore and in the harbour itself the shimmering wide ribbon of silver which was the reflection of the illumination of a cruise ship anchored there.

'Do you want to dance?' Jake put the question hesitantly, aware of how Dominie must be feeling.

But she agreed and they went to the terrace, where an orchestra was playing. A short while later they were having a quiet drink when Jake said,

'I've just spotted two people I knew a long while ago when I lived in New York. They must be here on holiday—perhaps they've come on the cruise ship. Do you mind if I go and have a few words with them?'

She smiled and said no, of course she didn't mind, and as her eyes were following him as he walked away she failed to see Rohan and Sylvia come and occupy a table at the other side of her. But she had not been alone many minutes when she glanced up to see Rohan standing there, faultlessly attired in white jacket and tie, and looking unfamiliarly pale around the mouth.

Her heart fluttered; her lips formed a nervous 'hello', but no sound issued from them. The amber eyes, strangely gleaming yellow in the soft artificial light, remained on her unblinkingly for a long moment before Rohan said, in tones as crisp as frost,

'Shall we dance, Dominie?'

Startled by the invitation, she rose mechanically, only to discover that her legs were like jelly beneath her. A swift glance around and she saw Sylvia, sitting alone, her eyes brittle, her pretty mouth pursed and her wide brow darkly furrowed.

'I—I—if you d-don't mind I'd rather not——' But Dominie was already in Rohan's arms and being swung away from her table. After a little while she ventured a glance from under her lashes; Rohan's face was an unsmiling mask, but when she examined the expression in his eyes her heart twisted in pain. He must be the most unhappy man present tonight, as she was the most unhappy woman. Fate ... Tears gathered in her eyes and she looked down, at the lapel of his jacket. He must not see those tears; she must be free to keep firmly to her resolve. Should he note her unhappiness he would without mercy force the truth from her. And he'd then say it didn't matter what she had done because it hadn't been her fault. The result would be that he would persuade her to marry him—oh yes, she admitted to herself that she would not be able to resist him, to combat his forceful personality—and for a while they would be deliriously happy. But when the first romantic weeks and months had passed he would begin to think, and to remember that his wife had killed his sister . . .

Dominie thought, 'The romance wouldn't ever pass, so why don't I take a chance?' But the next second she was telling herself firmly that no matter how deep Rohan's love for her might be, no matter how enduring, he must inevitably reach a point where memory brought back again and again the hateful truth. If only she herself could have kept the secret, could have married Rohan without his ever learning who she was, then there would never have been this unsurmountable barrier between them. But she could not; she knew herself too well to be deceived into the fact that she could live a lie. It would not be living a lie, Jake had maintained, but Dominie had her own high ideals and values, and to her way of thinking a deliberate suppression of the truth was tantamount to living a lie.

'Aren't you going to say anything to me, Dominie?' Rohan's quiet, accented voice cut into her thoughts and she glanced up at him.

'Is there anything to say?' she prevaricated, nerves tensed as with a turning of her head she sought the table to which Jake had gone. If only the music would stop, and if only Jake were there when it did—she would ask him to take her home at once.

'I suppose not,' with a sort of cold finality that made her wince with pain. 'No, I suppose there isn't anything more for you and me to say to one another.' He looked down and she saw the quiver to his mouth. 'Do you want me to take you back to your table?'

'Please.'

He escorted her back and then left her without a word. Tightly she gripped her hands together, inwardly crying out to herself. Why couldn't she take a chance! Why ... *why*!

Within a fortnight of arriving home she was working in an office, and trying to settle into a routine similar to that which she had known before taking that fateful cruise. Mavis and James had found a suitable house to buy just a week prior to Dominie's return and as they would be leaving her in about a month's time she decided she must be thinking about advertising for someone else to share her home, for the swiftly-rising expenses entailed in the running of it were more than she could manage alone.

Mavis had been curious regarding her sudden decision to come home, but at least Dominie was saved any embarrassing questions regarding her engagement, as she had not mentioned it in her letters to Mavis, deciding that she would do so only when the engagement was announced. How odd, Dominie mused one day when she was sitting alone having her tea in the neat little kitchen which in her absence Mavis had kept as immaculate as ever, that she had so many times had doubts and forebodings about the future. Like any other engaged girl she had tried to visualize her wedding day—the lovely white gown and the flower-bedecked church; the organ and the choir, the reception afterwards ... and then the longed-for moment of finding herself alone with her husband ... None of this could be brought into focus; a shadow always appeared and blotted it out. Obviously she had had a premonition of what was to happen; subconsciously she had known all along that something would occur to prevent the marriage taking place.

Little had she thought that she herself would be the one to break the engagement, forced to do so by the discovery that she was the woman responsible for the accident that had robbed Rohan of the sister he so dearly loved.

With a little sob she rose and, picking up the kettle, poured more water on to the tea-leaves already in the pot. It was Saturday afternoon and Mavis and James had gone off early, intending to spend the day in the garden of their new house, for the builders had left it in a most untidy state.

'We won't be back until dark,' Mavis had told her and Dominie had looked forward to a lonely day. She had tried to take her mind off her misery by finding work to do about the house; she had gone out and done some unnecessary shopping at the supermarket, buying for both the coming week and the next. And now she was trying to eat food for which she had no appetite at all. If only she could stop thinking of Rohan, then life would be much more bearable, but always it was his beloved face that rose between her and any other picture she might try to bring to mind. Even when Erica or Jake or the children intruded Rohan was always there too. Erica ... She would be on the island by now—settled in, in fact. Dominie recalled the lightness she had experienced when Erica had first visited Sunset Lodge; she knew now that it had resulted from the conviction that Erica and Jake would eventually get together. Well, in all probability they would get together, now that Erica was living in Jake's house. Dominie sincerely hoped they would be happy, for Erica had waited so long——

Her musings came to an abrupt halt as a car door slammed at the end of the short path leading to the lane. Rising, she went to the window; her eyes dilated and unconsciously she pressed a hand against her heart.

'Rohan!' Her heart thudded beneath her hand. Was he real?

He was striding towards the side door of the house, his eyes scanning the ground-floor windows as he did so. On seeing her he turned again, took some money from his pocket and paid the taxi driver, then came towards the door again. The knocker fell as she was about to open the door and she jumped nervously. What could he want? Had he learned the truth? Had Jake broken his promise——?

'Well, aren't you going to ask me in?'

The abrupt voice, the narrowed angry eyes, the compression of those sensuous lips ... Dominie said, her voice edged with fear,

'Wh-what d-do you want?'

Rohan's lips parted; she heard his teeth grit together. The door was pushed open and he entered, brushing past her and then waiting, until she had collected herself sufficiently to close the door.

'And now,' he said, glaring down at her in the dimness of the tiny hall, 'we'll talk! Is this where you were?' and without waiting for her answer he had entered the kitchen, where on a small formica-topped table her tea was laid.

'No—er—no. I—we usually sit in the other room.' She stopped, and passed a tongue over her dry lips. 'Rohan, why have you come?' Appealing tones, jerky and edged with tears; eyes that willed his own to lose that harsh forbidding light, a hand unconsciously pressed to her cheek. Rohan's mouth relaxed as he took in all these things. He shook his head in a gesture which denoted both censure and exasperation.

'Why have I come?' he repeated. 'Are you totally obtuse?—not that it wouldn't match your stupidity,' he added grimly, and pointed to a chair. 'Sit down; you look ready to faint!'

She remained on her feet, but put out a hand to the back of the chair, holding it as if she required support.

'You've discovered the truth,' she began, thoughts wildly confused because she could not believe that Jake had gone back on his word. 'You know ... know that I ...' Impossible to say it; her face puckered and she turned from him. 'I don't know why you've come, Rohan, but if it's to ask me to marry you, then the answer's no——' She got no further. Rohan gripped her shoulders, roughly bringing her round to face him.

'I haven't come to ask you to marry me. I've come to take my fiancée back home—to Windward Crest, where she belongs!' He gave her a little shake, as if he just had to, in order to relieve his feelings. But his face had softened and his hands on her arms became more gentle. 'You idiot, Dominie,' he said, a muscle throbbing in his neck, revealing the depth of his emotion. 'You ridiculous child——'

'Rohan,' she cut in urgently, 'I can't marry you with a shadow like that between us. Jake must have told you all, but he must also have explained that I told him I couldn't marry you without confessing who I really was, and if I did confess I couldn't marry you either, because although you'd agree that it wasn't my fault, the day would come when you'd begin to hate me.'

'It would? When?'

'When we had a tiff, perhaps——'

'We aren't going to have any tiffs,' he interrupted, astounding her now by his expression. His eyes were actually twinkling with amusement. 'No, my Dominie, we shan't have any tiffs, simply because you'll have more sense than to rub me up the wrong way, more especially, since you've learned a little about my temper. Incidentally,' he continued without allowing her to speak, 'it wasn't Jake who told me the story; it was Erica.'

'Erica?' she echoed blankly. 'I never told Erica anything.'

'No, but Jake did. He sent for her specially to repeat what you'd said, and then told her to come and tell it all to me.'

Dominie stared.

'That wasn't very nice of Jake—and there was no other reason for his sending for Erica?' she asked, for the moment diverted.

'Not at the time——'

'But the children. He required a nanny for them.'

'There was no need to send all that way just for a nanny. However, he admitted that he was a little interested in Erica, after what you had told him.' A slight pause and then, 'They're to be married in about a month. Erica's gone off to sell up her home and other belongings; she'll be back in time for our wedding. I promised to put it off until she returns.' So cool now, he appeared, and perfectly self-assured. But a move-

177

ment in his throat had not yet been brought under control.

'I can't marry you, Rohan.' Dominie had been some moments in making this statement, because of the pain it would cause Rohan, and of course herself, and because it would be far easier just to give up the struggle and allow him his own way ... and because she yearned to be in his arms ...

He looked at her intently through those shrewd and piercing eyes.

'You spoke a lot of rubbish just now about a shadow being between us——'

'It isn't rubbish!' she cut in urgently. 'It would always be there——'

'Will you be quiet, Dominie, and let me finish!' He glowered down at her and she said, catching at her dress in a little gesture of agitation he had seen before,

'I'm sorry, Rohan. I was just trying to make you understand.'

'And I'm trying to make you understand. Dominie,' he said in slow deliberate tones he would have used if speaking to a very young child, 'you had nothing to do with my sister's death.'

Silence. For one wild moment of joy she believed him and every cloud went from her eyes. But suddenly enlightenment dawned and she slowly shook her head.

'You're just saying that,' she stated with conviction. 'It won't work, Rohan ...' On noting the glowering expression that entered his eyes Dominie allowed her voice to trail away to a mere whisper.

'Dominie,' he said in a very soft voice, 'you really are asking for it. How far do you expect my patience to stretch? Have you given a thought to what I've taken from you?—to all the trouble you've caused me? You first of all treated me to your scorn and arrogance in that bower, accusing me of flirting before your eyes—which was a damned lie! You called me pompous; you jilted me, threw back my ring at me——'

'I never threw it——'

'Hold your tongue!' Subdued, Dominie hung her head, nervously twisting her fingers as Rohan continued, 'You allowed me to believe you preferred Jake to me, you've put me to all this trouble of coming here after you, and now you accuse me of lying!' He gritted his teeth. 'I've reached the end, Dominie. Try me one step further and you'll drive me to something I'll regret!'

'I'm sorry,' she hastened to say, his words beginning to register properly in her mind. 'About that scene in the arbour, Rohan,' she just had to add, 'it was all an act, necessary, as you should have seen if Erica told you the whole.'

'Of course I now know it was an act, but I didn't then. And in any case, does it make it any better, if it was an act?' he demanded wrathfully.

Dominie swallowed.

'Well . . . no.'

He looked at her for a space, then took something from his pocket and handed it to her, retaining something else in his hand.

'I rather thought you might suspect me of lying,' he said, 'so here's proof that you were not involved in that accident.'

'Proof?' Dazedly she looked at the paper as she took it from him. 'Proof . . . there can be no proof.' But she lowered her eyes to read, noting the rusty mark at one corner, made at some time or other by a paper-clip. 'Aged about sixty. Stout, double chin. Jet black hair obviously dyed——' She broke off, the glance she would have given Rohan transferred to the snapshot he held on his open palm. He flipped it over and she saw that the handwriting was the same as on the paper she had just been reading. Her heart gave a great bound, even though, as yet, she had not by any means grasped the whole of the unfolding miracle. 'It's a description of—of someone——'

'Of the woman who was driving the car. The man who witnessed the accident sent it to me, along with the picture of the spot where it happened. It was no good to me ... not at that time,' added Rohan significantly, his eyes on the paper, fluttering in her hand. 'It has certainly come in useful now,' he ended with a sort of grim triumph. 'You can scarcely refuse to believe me—unless, of course, you are able to identify yourself —I mean, the double chin and the dyed hair——'

'Rohan,' she interrupted in a fearful little voice he had never expected to hear, 'it all sounds very well, but I remember it all; I did as soon as I saw the snapshot of the place where the accident occurred. I must have been involved!'

Rohan set his mouth.

'Dominie, please don't start an argument over this. If you continue as you have been doing then I must accept that you really do want to call our marriage off——'

'Oh, but no!' The exclamation was out before she had time to think, and pretty colour flooded into her pale cheeks. Rohan's eyes softened as he noted this, but his voice was neither caressing nor tender, as she would dearly have liked it to be.

'That's something. We might, with my perseverence, make some progress after all.'

With her hands she made a little gesture of placation, but seconds later forgot all about it as she said, a clear vision rising up before her,

'I remember the screeching of brakes so well. And——' She stopped then and frowned. 'There were lights. And I do very clearly remember the man putting his head through the car window and saying ... saying I w-was drunk.'

Ignoring this latter sentence, Rohan seized on the one before it.

'Lights? What lights? You never mentioned lights to Jake.'

'No ... I didn't ...' Dominie knit her brows in concentration. 'There were coloured lights. I remember them now.' She looked up at him. His face was set in austere lines. 'Perhaps from a shop ...' She let her voice fade, allowing Rohan to say what was in her mind.

'There were no shops anywhere near this place. It was quiet, and very dark. It was a major road in relation to the other, but by no means *a* major road. On the contrary, it was just a country lane. Coloured lights,' he mused. 'Traffic lights?'

Her eyes widened.

'Yes, Rohan! Yes——' She stopped, shaking her head. 'But there were no traffic lights at that spot.'

'Therefore,' he cut in softly, 'whatever happened to you happened somewhere else. Jake told Erica that you weren't at all sure that this was the road you came out of, and it's my opinion that had you never seen this snapshot you would never have connected this particular place with anything you had done, and,' he added wrathfully, 'you wouldn't have acted in so precipitate a manner, flying from me as if the devil himself were after you!'

Dominie averted her head. She murmured, just for something to say,

'Perhaps you're right, Rohan.'

'I am right.' He frowned at her bent head. 'Jake told Erica that you maintained you had a lapse of memory on your way home. All drivers have lapses of memory. I drive regularly into Charlotte Amalie, as you know, but I don't note every curve and bend; every single landmark doesn't loom out at me and register. When I get to the end of a journey I couldn't describe what I saw on every inch of the way.'

'I understand that,' Dominie readily agreed. 'But, you see, it was those brakes—the terrible screeching— that kept coming back to me all the time, and if it hadn't been that my car was unmarked I'd have sworn I myself had been involved in an accident. When I saw that snapshot it all seemed to fit into place——'

'In other words you did manage to fit your unmarked car into an accident. Clever girl; go on.'

'I do realize that you consider me silly——'

'That's putting it mildly indeed. But I asked you to continue.'

'There isn't anything else. You know it all. I concluded that I was responsible for Alicia's death.'

An impatient click of his tongue was all the reaction she received to that for the moment. And then Rohan said,

'I rather think that all that happened in your case was that you almost shot the traffic lights at some place or another, and you jammed on your brakes—or you might even have actually shot them and someone else braked——'

'But the man. What about the man?'

Rohan's frown returned.

'If you were stopped at the lights he might have been asking for a lift. What exactly did he say to you?' Dominie was staring at him wide-eyed and he added, misinterpreting that stare, 'You don't remember? You told Jake that he said something more than the comment about your—er—intoxicated state.' The merest hint of humour touched his eyes as this was said.

'I do remember! Rohan—you're right; he *was* asking for a lift!' Her eyes shone suddenly as the last piece of the picture fell into place. She felt free—free! 'He tapped on the window and when I wound it down he asked if I was going past the railway station, and then he said, "Drunk! Never mind; I might be in a hurry to catch my train, but I'm not intending to risk my life to do it." And he repeated the word drunk again and again—at least, I think he did.'

'It doesn't matter.' Tenderness looked out from those amber eyes now, and Rohan took her hand in his. 'Stupid child,' he murmured as he brought her hand up to his lips. 'Jumping to a wild conclusion like that. Did it never occur to you that, having seen the snapshot, you immediately proceeded to build up your own picture of what happened during those lost few minutes? They'd been troubling you ever since that evening and, consciously or subconsciously, you had a deep desire to fill in those moments. When you saw that snapshot, Dominie, the only thing that came to you was the incident of the man putting his head through the window. From that you built up the most stupid picture and in view of the blanks still existing I'm amazed that Jake could accept that you were to blame for the accident. It's only now, during the past few minutes while we've been talking, that memory has been fully restored to you.' Rohan stopped and gave a small shrug. 'True, there's a bit missing because you're not sure about those screeching brakes, or about the particular place where you entered the main road, but these are of no matter. I myself favour the idea that you yourself applied the brakes on realizing you were about to drive on when the lights were against you.' He looked at her and shook his head in a little gesture of impatience. But his voice was gentle when he said, 'The important thing is that your mind has been put at rest by your remembering that the man merely wanted a lift from you, that he was not the witness to my accident.'

Dominie said nothing for a space, dwelling on what he had said, and recalling her own admittance that full memory had not returned on her seeing the snapshot. But when Jake said that the picture was that of the spot where the accident had occurred, and as she knew that Alicia was killed about the same time that she herself was returning from the mortuary, pieces of a picture seemed naturally to fall into place ... with a little manoeuvring from her, Dominie now admitted. But she had in fact built up her own picture, as Rohan had just explained.

'So it was all for nothing.' Dominie shuddered at the memory of all that they had both suffered; and it was so unnecessary, brought about by her stupidity in jumping to the wrong conclusion. She thought of the manner in which she spoke to him that day in the bower, when she had told him their engagement was at an end. Looking up at him now, with his face stern despite the slight relaxing of his mouth and jaw, she did wonder how she had had the temerity to adopt so scornful and arrogant an attitude towards him. 'I don't know how you can forgive me,' she uttered in a very small voice.

'I don't either,' came the unexpected agreement, and Dominie's lip trembled. His face softening miraculously, he said in low and tender accents, 'You must be something quite out of the ordinary, my darling, to be able to treat me like you have and get away with it.'

'I'm so sorry,' she whispered. 'At the time I was almost out of my mind over the whole business and I just had to give you up.'

'And a very good job you made of it. For a few minutes I was so mad I could have killed you. But I hadn't got far when I decided to turn back, unable to accept that you were really throwing me over, for I had been so sure of your love——' He stopped and frowned impatiently. 'No more of the past! The whole miserable business is finished with and won't ever be mentioned again by either of us. Understand?'

She nodded, swallowing the tight little lump in her throat as she thought of him coming back and finding her in Jake's arms.

'I'll never, never hurt you again ... not for one little second——' She got no further as she was swiftly caught into his arms and the rest was smothered by his kiss.

'My precious girl,' he whispered in the tenderest tone she had ever heard him use to her, 'my adorable angel...' He took her face between his hands and looked into her eyes; she caught her breath in wonderment, for never in the most intimate moments they had spent together had she seen so softened an expression on those stern and haughty features. 'I shall never let you out of my sight again, Dominie, I need you so——' His strong deep voice actually broke and in a little access of love she flung both her arms round his neck, went up on tiptoe, and pressed her lips to his.

'I love you,' she whispered simply, and tenderly gave him her lips again.

For a little while there was silence in the room as the pleasures of the moment occupied them both. But eventually Rohan spoke, imperiously telling her that she must pack right away and come back with him to St Thomas, back to the home which was now hers.

'Oh, but I can't go to Windward Crest immediately. I expect I can stay with Jake until we're married.'

'You're coming straight home,' he told her inflexibly. 'There are plenty of servants around to lend propriety to the situation.' His expression changed suddenly and he looked with deep tenderness into her eyes. 'Haven't I said I'm not letting you out of my sight again?' She nodded happily and Rohan went on to say that they would be married very soon anyway. 'I promised to wait till Erica's return, which should be in about a couple of weeks' time.'

'And I suppose she will then begin making arrangements for her own wedding?'

'That's right.'

'It all seems to have been done very quickly—I mean, Erica's not been on the island very long.'

'Not quite three weeks. I was away in New York when she arrived and didn't return until the day before yesterday. She and Jake seemed to be very much in love—but of course, you already knew that Erica cared for Jake.'

'Yes; it was Jake I was worried about.'

'Then you need worry no more. He's a very happy man, Dominie, and both he and Erica say they have you to thank.'

Dominie opened her mouth to protest, then changed her mind, saying instead,

'You, Rohan ... you didn't waste much time either.' This sounded out of place, once it had been voiced, and a soft flush of embarrassment rose to Dominie's face.

Rohan laughed and flicked her cheek caressingly.

'Erica came over soon after my return, and the whole absurd story came to my ears. Had you been anywhere at hand I'd have beaten you, I was so angry at your jumping to such a ridiculous conclusion. However, you were quite out of reach and so escaped my wrath. But be warned, my girl, and don't let your imagination run away with you like that again.' He was laughing with his eyes as he spoke, and the French accent seemed very pronounced. Dominie caught her breath at the attractiveness of him. 'I managed to get a seat on the first available plane and so here I am—with my own dear girl.' His tones dropped to a very tender note and his gaze was serious now. For a while he had been fingering a thin gold chain which Dominie wore around her neck, and now he slipped a thumb beneath it with the intention of bringing to light whatever hung on the end of it.

'I'm quite unable to contain my curiosity a moment longer, my love. What have you got down there, so close to your heart?'

A small embarrassed smile fluttered.

'Guess,' she bade him, and his brow knit thoughtfully.

'A locket with my picture in it. You must have come by a snapshot somehow—from Jake, probably. He's always busy with that camera of his.'

'It isn't a locket. Have another guess.'

'My imagination runs only to a locket...' Tugging gently, he brought up her engagement ring. Dominie had had it repaired and cleaned and now it lay in the palm of her fiancé's hand, warm from its contact with her body. Unfastening the chain, he slipped it off and dropped the chain on to the table. 'My own dear sweet darling...' The words, spoken with such tender emotion, trailed away on a husky note and Dominie saw to her astonishment that his mouth actually quivered in a little convulsive movement. Taking her finger he slid the ring on to it, then enclosed her small hand in his, gripping it hard. Too full to speak, Dominie could only lift her eyes to his, silently conveying all that was in her heart.

Harlequin Plus

A WORD ABOUT THE AUTHOR

For Anne Hampson, writing is more than just a livelihood. It is also an exciting hobby. Time and again she travels to foreign shores, where she mingles with the people who live there, gets to know them and even consigns a few interviews to tape. She takes a great many snapshots, buys dozens of postcards and collects maps of the area. Then, when she returns home to England, she makes notes, files them according to category and begins to write.

But long before Anne became a published author, she led a varied and often challenging existence, gathering a wealth of experiences along the way. Her working life began when she was very young—she left school at fourteen—and she has done everything from running a cafe to delivering milk at five-thirty in the morning. This last job was arranged so that she could return to school, a teacher-training college, as a "mature" student. And before deciding to write fulltime, Anne taught for a number of years.

Anne Hampson likes to describe herself as a collector; not only of maps and picture postcards, but of rocks, fossils, antiques and experiences.

FREE!
Romance Treasury

**A beautifully bound,
value-packed,
three-in-one
volume of romance!**

Romance Treasury

An exciting opportunity to collect treasured works of romance! Almost 600 pages of exciting romance reading in each beautifully bound hardcover volume!

You may cancel your subscription whenever you wish! You don't have to buy any minimum number of volumes. Whenever you decide to stop your subscription just drop us a line and we'll cancel all further shipments.

FREE GIFT!
Certificate and Subscription Reservation

Mail this coupon today to
Harlequin Reader Service

In the U.S.A.
1440 South Priest Drive
Tempe, AZ 85281

In Canada
649 Ontario Street
Stratford, Ontario N5A 6W2

Please send me my **FREE** Romance Treasury volume. Also, reserve a subscription to the new **Romance Treasury** published every month. Each month I will receive a Romance Treasury volume at the low price of $6.97 plus 75¢ for postage and handling (total—$7.72). There are no hidden charges. I am free to cancel at any time, but if I do, my **FREE** Romance Treasury volume is mine to keep, without any obligation.

NAME _____
(Please Print)

ADDRESS _____

CITY _____

STATE/PROV. _____

ZIP/POSTAL CODE _____

Offer expires October 31, 1982
Offer not valid to present subscribers.

DB494

Lying to him took
the utmost courage

"I'm not willing to take the risk,"
Dominie said resolutely, half turning
from a bewildered Rohan. "Our
engagement's off and—and here's
your ring." She held it out, not daring
to glance at him.

"Are you out of your mind?" he
demanded, his voice faintly harsh,
edged with hurt.

"I can't marry you," she said shakily.

"*Can't?*" he echoed swiftly, his amber
eyes intent and deeply searching.

"I d-don't love you," Dominie
explained through whitened lips.
"You'll just have to accept that."

Suddenly the ring slipped from her
fingers. She bent to retrieve it, then
saw a perfectly shod foot come close
to her hand. Dazed, she watched as
Rohan ground the ring into the soil,
the gold twisting under the weight
of his fury....

ANNE HAMPSON
is also the author of these

Harlequin Presents

ANNE HAMPSON

windward crest

Harlequin Books

TORONTO • LONDON • LOS ANGELES • AMSTERDAM
SYDNEY • HAMBURG • PARIS • STOCKHOLM • ATHENS • TOKYO

Harlequin Presents edition published April 1982
ISBN 0-373-10494-4

Original hardcover edition published in 1973
by Mills & Boon Limited